Calamity

By D.H.

Hope you enjoy!
DH

Flammable Penguins Publishing
Copyright © 2021 Daphne D'Haenens

D.H. Dhaenens

Calamity at Cattori V

The right of Daphne D'Haenens to be identified as the Author of the Work has been asserted by her in accordance with Copyright, Designs and Patents Act 1988.

First published in Great Britain in 2021
by FLAMMABLE PENGUINS PUBLISHING

Apart from any use permitted under UK copyright law, this publication may only be reproduced, stored, or transmitted, in any form, or by any means, with prior permission in writing of the publishers or, in the case of reprographic production, in accordance with the terms of the licences issues by the Copyright Licensing Agency.

All characters in this publication are fictitious and any resemblance to real persons, living or dead, is purely coincidental.

ISBN 978-0-9956967-4-7

FLAMMABLE PENGUINS PUBLISHING
International House
24 Holborn Viaduct
CITY OF LONDON
London EC1A 2BN

www.flammablepenguins.com

For Claire, the best wife any tiny gay person could have hoped for.

Thank you to Bettina,
my supportive and stylish friend,
and to Steph, for their chaotic inspiration.

Prologue
The Abduction, Meeting Tommy

As usual with this ridiculous bullshit, it came from the fucking stars.

It was dark, his path mostly illuminated by the stars above and some small lights every few yards. Crickets chirped, their noise becoming louder and then quieter again as he passed by. The dusty road had a pleasant crunch beneath his feet.

The young man felt his feet lift from the ground. Yet there was no fear, his senses were sharp, and he could feel the air push past. For a minute, it felt like he was floating. It was kind of a pleasant sensation, and if he looked down, he could see his footprints in the dirt road end mid-stride.

That was when the illusion gave way, rippling as if seen through the heat of a flame. This was not a dream.

"DO NOT BE ALARMED, HUMAN." A voice boomed.

He blinked and gasped. "Wha... Who's there?" He called out and looked around. The vision of the road was entirely gone now. All he could see was the interior of a spaceship.

At least, that was the closest thing it reminded him of. He had never travelled, as he had been born on a remote human colony, not Earth. Once, during his induction tour, he had been on the inside of an Infinity ship. That had been small compared to the massive steel structure he was currently in. It would have seemed like an impossibly long and large hallway if it hadn't been for the pillars with strange writings and symbols.

"What is this?" He repeated. "Who's there?"

"WE ARE THE ATLANTANS, HU-"

"And you can stop shouting. I'm right here!" His senses were being assaulted enough without the loud booming which seemed to vibrate every fibre of his being.

There was a moment of silence, perhaps a quick squeak as something seemed to be adjusted.

"We are the Atlantans."

"Right. Never heard of you." The statement held more bravado than he felt. In fact, he'd never felt very brave, but somehow he knew that his self-confidence would play a role in him getting home.

"We have selected you for your admirable traits."

"I think you chose wrong, whatever this is for. I'm a fat lazy desk jockey who makes a decent paella. That's about it." At least they were straight to the point. Still, he had no idea if this was a dream or not.

"You sell yourself for a gas giant when you are a habitable

planet."

The human frowned as the alien used the Terran lingo used on Cattori Five.

"You studied us." It was as much a statement as a question.

"Yes, to find you. We know you are the correct one for the task we have at hand." The disembodied voice delivered this final line as a pair of doors slid open.

The alien was relatively diminutive, less tall than a human, and appeared unspeakably frail. Their skin seemed transparent, and he knew from looking at the weak body he could kill them just by hugging them too hard. Then again, who was the alien on his planet? He was a human but born on a different planet. Did that make him an alien to the world his mother was from?

Later, he realised his perceived physical prowess had played a role in how they had chosen him, but right now, there was too much to process.

"I am Parvas." The alien's small mouth uttered with a heavy accent that had not been audible in the booming PA voice.

"I am... Ah, nevermind." He replied before realising they knew his name already. They seemed to know everything. But what else could one say to an alien race's first representative? What if he said the wrong thing? He could not get a Warning on his planet, or he'd never get promoted.

"We have chosen you. You will become our ambassador."

"What? I... No." He shook his head. "I never applied for this. What are you even trying to pull here?" He asked.

"We are... trying not to pull?" The alien frowned. Or perhaps he just imagined that because the being's facial expressions were just... skewered somehow. It was the lack of eyes and eyebrows. It was freaky and hard to read at the same time. Though they probably did have eyes – they were just hidden under the transparent skin. There were three black orbs on the upper half of the face's surface, which he guessed they used to see.

"Does earth know you exist?"

"Probably not. We prefer to remain unknown and to use others we send as our ambassadors. You will help us in our first step."

He hadn't understood much of that first step. "I don't..."

"You don't need to. You're just a part of our plan, and you will be brilliant." Parvas was probably the best at reassurances because he immediately felt some of the stress fall away.

"Okay." Was his underwhelming response; he had no mind for elaborate ceremony. Alien or human.

"You will be our guest for a little while," Parvas said. "You'll want for nothing."

And Tommy had just nodded. Over that week, the alien had kept his word.

Chapter One

One Year Later

Fun fact: There is no such thing as rush hour in a penal colony.

Tommy strolled out of his apartment building on the main street of Centauri Bridge, a central area of the second-largest city on the planet. It was where all the pencil pushers and service providers like himself lived and worked. The streets were straight and clean and at six am, the street lights complemented the light from the rising sun, which was just starting to warm the day up. The crossing lights blinked in soothing warm colours, wishing pedestrians a safe crossing in a gentle voice. Even the warm breeze was pleasant. Bikes and vehicles resembling kick scooters patiently waited for the lights to turn. After all, running the light was a serious crime.

Many things on the planet were serious crimes: jaywalking, driving or owning unauthorised motorised vehicles, fighting, arguments, smuggling unlicensed goods...

Cattori Five was a penal planet with a giant sun, providing

it with a gentle, warm climate. It was considered a comfortably habitable planet.

The sheer distance from any other systems rendered it undesirable for most people. It took almost three years to travel here from Earth. So it was a perfect place to put people you didn't like.

Tommy paused at the Pioneers Statue, two men and two women, looking much more stately than they probably had in life. Reasonably they would have been filthy without the noble fashion. Expected to be fighting over the meagre supplies they had been dropped off with. Still, they had defied expectations and started farms and ranches. There had almost been a little town by the time earth had bothered to notice how they were doing.

From then on, they had decided to really help out these poor people. Building materials had been brought in, and they had erected buildings and parks and brought with them the Culture of Kindness.

The pioneers were still the real heroes to everyone who landed here, of course, but Tommy guessed it was nice to have heating and office buildings. The Culture also encouraged remembrance of the pioneers, so they had not become some sort of martyrs. Just a normal part of history. Not much more, nothing less. It gave him the shivers thinking how much say these people actually got in planetary policy and the history books. Everything was designed; nothing had happened organically.

Calamity at Cattori V

There was no official record of where the first farms had been formed, but Tommy guessed they had been razed over to place a parking lot or some other functional requirement.

Tommy stopped at the street crossing, eyes glancing around for the signal. It looked about to turn from the number of people waiting. And it did turn, briefly green, before slamming back to red. Tommy blinked. He'd only taken a few paces forward when the scuffling back onto the pavement began. A light turning back could only mean one thing.

"We've got a runner!" Someone grinned in front of him as a man ran down the road in front of them. Three enforcement agents ran after the man, calling out.

"Get out of my fucking way, native!" The fugitive shoved Tommy and kept running.

Even that encounter had slowed him down enough for the agents to catch up and shove the man down to the ground, stolen goods falling to the ground. Some stolen goods exchanged hands, and one of the officers seemed to put something away in his own pockets. The officer glared around challenging, but Tommy and many others simply looked away as if they had seen nothing. Soon life would continue on as before, and it was best to pretend you didn't see anything out of the ordinary. One didn't want to end up in one of the secret prisons on this planet.

Native. Tommy hated that. He knew he was different from

the others, and the fact he chose his own clothing rather than wear what was assigned to him made him stand out. "Native" was a slur thrown at people from Earth who had come here voluntarily and basically for anyone who wasn't here because of a crime.

Slowly the tense atmosphere let up. The excited whispers stopped, there was no shuffling and rubbernecking anymore, and the select few with communication devices started to check those to fill up the moments until the light would turn. The street was cleared, and the light turned green again, allowing the flow of pedestrians to restart.

The streets were laid out like modern Earth streets but were more of a clean imitation without the details filled in. He remembered the photos of Earth he'd seen in classes. Wide pavements and empty streets. The stores only stocked local goods produced outside of the main cities, and the coffee was homegrown and not that great. The tea harvests were much better, so it was only Earth-loving yuppies who dared ask the tea stands for the brown brew.

Tommy continued on, a cup of tea now in his own hands as he made his way into the building where he worked. His heels clicked softly on the tiled floor, a rhythmic beat accompanying him.

Outside, the street lights turned off with a soft click, and the PA system on the main square continued to wish everyone a good morning as the city transitioned into day mode. People briefly looked up but then, like Tommy, put their heads back down and continued their day. It was best not to be late for work or act too suspiciously, after all.

"Good morning, Tommy. You have twenty-six unread emails." The AI announced to him as he walked into the office. It was a slightly newer one than the one he had in his own living quarters and therefore a bit more eloquent, but the message was a downer just the same.

"Thanks, Belinda. I just got in." He couldn't help the snark, and as soon as he heard it in his own voice, he paused. He could almost hear the AI's gears grinding, calculating, reminding itself how many times before he had been grumpy. Finally, the AI spoke again.

"Of course, Tommy. Please don't forget your health check later today! I hope you got your weight down as the doctor requested!"

"Thanks, Belinda." This time he kept his voice flat. The receptionist giggled at the interaction between them, and he just shrugged it off. Public mention of his weight was still better than an Official Scolding, which could lead to an Official Warning. To have three Official Warnings was terrible. Some speculated it meant time in the jails outside of the cities, helping the farmers on the field. It was not where a city boy like him wanted to be. Especially as he was, as they said, a 'native'.

It usually helped in his favour that he had not been

convicted of any crime. There was a small minority of them on the planet, most contractors and peacekeepers working for the private Centauri Care Concern, Earth officials and ambassadors. Finally, there was him and about thirty-seven other unlucky souls who had been born on the planet.

His mother, Chris, had been pregnant or had become pregnant on the way to the colony when she had been convicted of Grand Theft. She had loved her diamonds, but she was a kind woman. On this planet, without many material distractions, she had righted her life. She had become an agricultural expert, helping the farmers design planting schedules that worked for this planet's particular climate. Many plants depended on their home planet's natural rhythms, and this one had barely any native species. Last he had heard from her, she lived near a tea field, creating a new strain of chamomile that would hopefully take. This planet needed a chill pill. Tommy continued towards his desk and sat down.

Most of his work was service and peacekeeping related. As he had no criminal record, he had been allowed to join the Centauri Care Concern through the fast track application process. His job was mostly to check in on new arrivals and help them settle in. They would be shown their new accommodation and how to look for a job, or start their own (authorised) business. It was tough to integrate into a society where even being mopey could get you a Scolding from an overly happy AI. It still sat badly with him that he had been unable to control himself and had almost reached a Scolding. He did not want to be singled out for any reason. A whir came from the corner as the printer spun to life. Printed copies of the case files spewed out the machine. Details of the new arrivals he was greeting. His new cases to help integrate, so they didn't become Anomalies who needed to be Scolded. He set to work going through his emails and morning routine.

"Hi, Tommy." The AI chirped again. "Your partner will be waiting in the main lobby. You are authorised to use vehicle pod B5 for your trip to the arrivals spaceport. Please have a safe trip."

"Thank you, Belinda." He scrolled through his emails and made sure to read the message about his new partner.

"I'll be there shortly." He shut off the screen on his desk and made his way down again, throwing the empty teacup neatly in one of the recycling bins.

Unbeknownst to the system, he was already more of an Anomaly than anyone would ever know.

Chapter Two
The New Guy

Tommy leaned against the elevator's cold metal wall, watching the numbers descend the shaft down to the pod yard.

"Hey, Tommy. Did you see the runner this morning?" Lion asked with a grin. His pearly whites contrasted with his olive skin. The grin was infectious. Lion was probably more popular with the ladies with his brown hair and rich maroon eyes than he ever was.

The two had only been working together for a week or two, but his new partner was easy-going, and Tommy could get along with him.

"Yeah, I was waiting for the light to turn when enforcement tackled him."

"Wow. Front row seats, huh."

"I guess." Tommy shrugged and walked around the pod to check it. It looked more like a small smart-terrain car, with big wheels to tackle the occasional out of city terrain, but they just called them pods over here. Car did not seem like the correct term for what looked like the angry bastard child of a Mars rover and a city car. The bureau only had three of these orbs.

"So, what's it like?" Lion shrugged off his brown leather jacket to get into the pod. He wasn't sure why the other insisted on wearing that thing. It was pretty warm here most of the time.

"Mmm?" Tommy looked up as he walked around the vehicle to get to the steering side. Though he had a suspicion of what the man was about to ask him.

"You're a non-convict, right? What's it like living between all of... us?" He gestured, and Tommy pushed his shoulders back. They were always curious about that. What it was like to spend your entire life here. Maybe because they had the same future ahead of them.

"I don't think about it much." Tommy had to admit after a pause. "My mother always said this place is much safer than Earth, so I never... really realised, I guess?" He shrugged.

"And you never committed a crime yourself? Nothing... even a lil dodgy?" Lion smirked.

Tommy sighed and looked over. "I have one Warning on my record. I disappeared for a week or so and failed to give a satisfactory answer as to where I was. If I don't get another warning for five years, it'll be taken off."

"Whoa, you gotta..."

"We have a job to do," Tommy said curtly.

Disappearing for a week was almost impossibly hard, so he knew why he was curious. Tommy had no magical clues for him and really didn't want to get either of them in trouble talking about this stuff, either. The only reason he had told him was that he had asked about it, and lying requires forethought.

"It's a bit of a way to the new arrivals hub. It's out of town after all." He added kinder, not wanting to seem rude. This whole place's vibe had probably had more of an effect on him than on anyone else.

"Of course." Lion seemed to reign himself in. "This is my first time greeting new arrivals; what are they like?" He politely changed the subject. In the short time they'd worked together, it had mostly been desk work, so this was a nice change.

He tapped in his access code and waited for the pod to open up as he thought about his answer.

"Confused. They've been on a ship for a long time, so this is the first solid ground they encounter in a while. Grieving, often. The long trip gives them a bit of time for that, but once they hit here and it sinks in just how far away from everything they are..." Tommy shook his head. "It's a long way, and many don't think they'll make it here. So when they do, it's a shock. You probably felt the same when you landed. The best thing to do is to get them set up in a house and offer them some kindness. Once they see this place isn't all bad, they generally follow along and play by the rules." Tommy concluded. That, so far, had been his experience at least.

Banished to a distant star, a death sentence, at least from the point of view of those on Earth. It was the worst punishment the judiciary could dish out. However, Tommy had read about actual executions done on Earth in the past. Non-violent offenders usually didn't land here unless they had been convicted multiple times. His partner had managed to get a position with the peacekeeping squad, so it was probably a non-violent offence, or nobody had been hurt.

The vehicle opened up as he took him in.

"Come on, ask. I've been waiting for it," Lion said patiently.

He rolled his eyes. "Okay. What are you here for?" Cattori Five etiquette dictated you didn't ask what someone else was in for. Unless they gave permission.

"Kidnapping. Don't make that face. The hostage was fine, but we grabbed a rich broad from the upper class. The fancy lawyers pushed for maximum punishment. So here I am." He clambered into the vehicle with the practised grace of someone who had been used to cars.

"So... how did you get a job with peacekeeping so fast? You've been here for less than a decade, no?"

"My skills," Lion strapped himself in. "I was a detective. Don't ask how I made the leap from law enforcement to kidnapping. I'm still trying to figure that one out myself."

Tommy chuckled and entered the car. "Deal. Won't ask if you won't ask about me going MIA."

"I've got my money on alien abduction," Said Lion. "Those Lhoorlians are a kinky bunch, I've heard."

Tommy laughed. It was true the Lhoorlian homeworld was the closest non-Terran settlement, but it was still a year away. A long way, even if you managed to get off the planet.

"I doubt they'll travel all year just for my sexy curves and then not let me remember it." He wiggled his ass until it was comfortable on the small chair. The AI was right; he did need to lose weight. He was tall but also big, but it was more dad bod than actually intimidating.

"Who knows. Have you met them?"

"A Lhoorlian? Once. One of their ships crash-landed when I was a teenager. It was chaos." He took a deep breath and started the vehicle as soon as he had his seatbelt on.

"Fuck. Did they live?"

"Oh yeah. They're tough to kill. In the end, Earth and Lhoorl worked together long enough to get them off the planet. They were... well. They lived up to their reputation."

"Fucking and fighting."

Tommy tapped his nose in agreement. The engine of the little pod revved up as they left the centre of town. Perhaps childishly, Tommy usually revelled in the jealous stares of onlookers. Most of them had had cars at home and were not really fond of losing their independence to trams and bikes.

"How long..."

"About 45 minutes. Then we bring them to their new homes." He patted the dashboard of the pod. It could stretch out to reveal four more seats, a little cramped but adequate.

He nodded. "You're the expert."

Tommy chuckled. "Just doing my job." He sat back and opened up the case files of the new arrivals. Flipping through the pages, he counted three cases assigned to him today. The first two were drug offenders, but the last file did not have much information besides a name and race.

"Oh, crap."

"What?" Lion craned his neck to try and see what had his partner on edge.

"It's a Lhoorlian," Said Tommy.

"What?!" Lion took the file from his hands. The car just kept up its leisurely 60 kilometres per hour, but Tommy wished he could reverse it.

"Cattori Five is not equipped for prisoners of war!"

"We're not at war with them either. Do you think his homeworld knows?" He wondered.

"Probably not. They prefer to drop their criminals out of spaceships." Lion shook his head.

"I thought that was an urban myth!" Gasped Tommy.

"Oh, no. It's true. The worst part is the criminals don't die, at least not right away. They just... float through space until they starve and go into hibernation. It's worse than this," Lion gestured out the window to the clean city outside.

"There's a lot that's worse than this," Tommy said. "Maybe he just jaywalked or something." He tried to lift the mood.

"Jaywalking doesn't get you sent here," He replied darkly.

"In the end, it's not our problem, yeah? We just make sure he has a roof over his head. That's it." His eyes darted around as they neared the giant spaceport.

Chapter Three
Quiet Drive

The spaceport was probably the most massive structure on the planet. It was well guarded with a giant fence around it and armed Centauri Care Concern guards standing outside the main gate to keep out trespassers. If he strained, he could see the snipers with the laser-guided rifles on the top of the wall, which lay about a metre behind the fence. There were probably more guards than he could see as well. It was all part of the security theatre. Show them only half of the actual force you had protecting the place. Though he only knew this because he worked for the company. His security clearance was just high enough to attend such meetings. He showed his ID to the guard and nodded for Lion to do the same.

Lion pulled on the cord that held his ID card and sighed. After a minute, the gates opened for them. Due to the pod's size and transparency, they were spared an inspection upon entering. Still, it was very likely they would be checked when leaving. The guards quickly glanced over the pod before waving them through, one hand always on their weapons.

"Someone's on edge," Lion said softly. "Think they know?"

"Most definitely," Said Tommy. "They get briefed on these things."

Lion nodded. "Great. Bunch of nervous soldiers with guns and a spaceship with convicts that's about to land. What could go wrong?"

"I'm sure they could find you a bulletproof vest if you don't trust their aim." Tommy raised an eyebrow. The pod was bulletproof, and he didn't intend to spend too much time outside of it, so he was not too worried. These pickups usually went fine. Staying calm counted for a lot when dealing with people trying to come to grips with a new situation. Some were angry. Some were sad, but they rarely took it out on him as he was one of the first people they met who would be kind and help them out. Even in his own small borough, his position earned him respect.

The little pod neatly rolled itself to the front of the arrival hall. The door opened, and Tommy got out, stretching his legs out with a groan. The pod's seats were a bit small for his size. Anyway, he preferred walking. After giving himself that moment, he reached down into the pod and pressed a button on the dashboard.

The pod closed itself and then started whirring before stretching out the overlapping glass plates. The pod had looked most like, well, an orb. That orb now stretched out like a lazy cat in the sun extending until it was more wormlike. Seats started unfolding from the floor, making room for a total of six people.

"That shit still amazes me." Lion shook his head. "Had you told me the penal colony would have such advanced tech..."

"It's a second-to-last-generation model, but it does the trick." Tommy nodded. "Companies give the colony handouts all the time, but CCC can buy its own stuff." Tommy continued. "Not to mention experimental stuff they want to test out somewhere else." He added with a chuckle, remembering all the different development iterations of the traffic pod.

The Centauri Care Concern was making a killing managing the colony for the government. As long as there weren't any riots and the Earth officials coming to do inspections were safe, the government was happy to pay. Earth issued subsidies, but they still let CCC monetise the private prison planet however CCC saw fit.

Most penal colonists worked for CCC in one way or another, whether in their factories or in their offices. Wages weren't high, but life here was cheap. Tommy earned just over Earth minimum wage by Earth standards, but he was squarely upper middle class on Cattori Five.

Lion nodded. "Uhuh." He said and then turned around as a chime announced the arrival of a ship. Guards and snipers started tensing up. Tommy could just feel it from the sudden tangible tension in the air. He'd seen all of this before.

The ship came in for the landing, and Tommy nodded to the observation deck.

"Come on. Let's go see it land." He walked into the brutalist building and towards the upper floors. Its concrete fingers reaching up into the sky as if to grasp it. Lion sped up the stairs, but Tommy had to pace himself to not be out of breath by the time they hit the top floor.

As usual, the observation deck was empty except for one guard dressed in fatigues squawking commands into his radio whenever there was anything to report. The spaceport was based on a civilian port, but there had been tweaks. Floor to ceiling glass in the hall allowed for viewing but it was reinforced. Many of the areas which would have served as food halls and news kiosks were closed off and secured. There were no hiding spots or alcoves in case anyone managed to get in. Unless you were supposed to be on a ship or at this spaceport, you were not getting in.

One day, Tommy thought. One day he would board a ship off of this planet. It was rare, but for the ones like he who had been born here and were not convicts, it was possible. It just took a lot of paperwork, time and money.

"So, did you come on one of those?" Tommy asked, looking at the descending spaceship. It was an Infinity

3000, one of the more common long-distance models available.

"Yeah. It was... Pretty comfortable, really. You can stuff about fifty people on there, but on the flight here, there were maybe seven, crew included. Can stretch your legs. I once wandered around for a few hours and didn't see anyone."

Tommy chuckled. The large ship slowly descended and breached the field around the planet. From that point on, any radio signals outwards would be blocked until the ship hit the atmosphere again. This was the part where everyone got nervous and trigger happy, and Tommy was glad to be up here.

The large ship briefly blocked anything within their field of view as it descended. Though the design was reminiscent of the original space shuttle, this was a lot thicker and more prominent. It was powered by a number of massive engines working overtime to slow the ship down.

It took only minutes for the ship to come in and land. Several safety checks were done while the engines powered down, the noise of it almost deafening. It was always a humbling sight.

From the ship, a metal tube telescoped out towards the floor. This port did not have facilities for ships without their own walkways. Guards walked out first, taking point at the bottom of the ramp before radioing permission for the door to open and the passengers to descend—all the while shouting directions to the stunned newcomers.

Tommy shook his head. Within ten minutes, these people would be going from military personnel shouting orders at them to him trying to establish something akin to friendship. For some, the culture shock was so strong, they became clingy and started seeing him as their only friend. Other people reacted in less predictable ways.

"I don't think you were here when I landed," Said Lion.

"Probably not. I only started getting these about a year ago," Said Tommy. He was young, but around here, you had to pull your weight from a young age. His twentieth birthday was only six months away, and then in eighteen months, he would be allowed to drink after he helped convicted criminals settle in. Lucky him. He glanced over to Lion, who seemed to be getting more nervous by the second.

"Relax. People can tell if you're freaking out, and it won't put them at ease. It'll be fine." If anything, he knew how to deal with people now. Even if he was almost a kid compared to the man next to him.

Lion finally nodded and stopped picking at his thumb. "Alright. Ah." He saw the three come down the walkway. The first was a tall man with a broken nose and thick curly dark hair. He glanced back into the spaceship but then walked on. Behind him, a shorter man with a mohawk and a babyface. Lastly, the Lhoorlian.

"You can always tell which one's the Lhoorlian." Lion said.

Tommy rolled his eyes. "It's not hard. It's the one with the long hair." In Lhoorlian society, long hair was a sign of status, of fighting ability. If you could fight well enough to be alive with long hair whipping around your face, that was a sign you probably shouldn't be messed with.

"This one's either gotten a haircut or is low ranking." Lion moved his head to the side.

The man's blonde hair was barely down to his shoulders, a small braid keeping the front part out of his face. His face had the markings of a Lhoorlian soldier on the side of the emperor. Fresh out of battle, it seemed. The marks usually disappeared after a few months. His fingernails were long, with almost talon-like nails. He also stood just slightly taller than humans, towering over his fellow passengers.

"I hear they eat humans raw," Lion said.

Tommy shivered but recomposed himself. "Don't be stupid. They cook human meat first."

"I still can't believe they sent him here."

"Believe it and do your job." Tommy turned away to go down the stairs. It was time to help get them settled.

Chapter Four
History Lesson

Cattori Five did not start its history as Cattori Five. The first discovery of the planet was widely celebrated. It was one of the first Goldilocks planets to be found within reach of Earth. Early probes had taken photos that had been spread worldwide as if it was a second chance for the entire world. Ambitious entrepreneurs made plans to fund settlements. For a while, there was a petition to name it Hope.

And then the relativistic travel time became too much. From Earth, the trip with the faster than light probe had seemed perfectly reasonable. Faster than light ships, however, had not been rated for human transport yet. The only ships that could make the long haul journey were the large, uncomfortable cargo ships used to mine moons.

Suddenly, any potential colonists ummed and arred at the prospect of spending three years on a slow ship with only each other for company and colonisation plans were put off.

Then the real cinch came with the discovery of the

Lhoorlian homeworld less than a year's travel away from the planet. Even quicker with the faster than light travel ships the aliens had and were unwilling to trade to Earth.

Lhoorl had a bit of a reputation on Earth. Most of it was true.

The Lhoorlian race was constantly at war with itself and others. Their system of government was fragile, with one emperor trying to rule an entire planet. Most shockingly, the world had a small human population. Early Russian cosmonauts who had been presumed lost in space had crash-landed on the planet and had integrated to the point where there were few pureblood humans left. Most had mingled with the humanoid aliens over time.

We've had to loosely translate some terms that have no real equivalents in Terran to explain the war.

Their current war revolves around three factions.

The largest group, the imperialists, believe the current and ruling emperor should have all power and that he is the one true ruler, his bloodline providing a successor. They believe that this approach works best and frees up resources and time for scientific research. Despite their reputation for bloodlust and war, they are actually very well versed in science and research.

The second faction supports a demarchy, dividing the government into sections. This includes a lottery to decide rulers every few years and to split up the large planet into smaller areas to rule. They admit this would lead to more strife and require more manpower to arrange these lotteries and help the day-to-day rule of the chosen ones. They, however, argue that it would be fairer.

The third group is not so much considered a party as they are a minority and have no strong or at least practical way to organise the rule of the planet. The anarchists want to raze it all and start afresh, but this includes murdering everyone who is not on their side. Both other parties fear them.

Lhoorlians are also very humanoid. Panspermic theories had apparently been spot on. Lhoorlians are taller, easily over two metres tall, with claw-like hands and larger eyes. They are tough, hard to kill, and hold a grudge like no other. While some speculated they had evolved along the same lines as humans, they are often spotted running on all fours. When on their best behaviour, however, they easily pass for humans.

At the same time, they have a very advanced culture with significant innovations in the way they observe stars and systems and very well developed space travel technologies. Their grasp of exobiology, exo-geography and weather systems is unparalleled. Earth's governments were just waiting for a few months, or hopefully years, of peace. Whatever time period would be long enough to negotiate the trade between their worlds to hopefully acquire some faster ships. For now, Earth's knowledge of the aliens was spotty, mostly happening through exchanges with scientists whenever there was a moment of peace and probes circled the planet. Lhoorlian scientists revelled in the fact that they could show off new knowledge and trade it for Earth facts through the common language of Russian, which they had learned from their local humans. Some had even started learning other human languages. So far, no humans had visited the planet due to the dangerous political climate, but the Russian Federation keeps proudly proclaiming how one day they would have the first embassy on Lhoorl.

Early terraforming machines were sent to Cattori Five in the meantime, mostly to test the technology, but their progress had been slow. The fauna and flora on the planet had been abundant, and the first few machines had been swallowed whole by swamps and whatever the planet's equivalent of rainforest was. Even now, outside of the well-tended gates, nature was still a force to be reckoned with.

The Centauri Care Concern, however, had approached the problem differently. Why not build prisons on the newly discovered planet? Earth was overcrowded. The prisoners could help tend the colony until the travel distance was more manageable for people with clear consciences. The whole concept had been sold as using prisoners to become the guardians for the planet. Earth didn't really believe in it, but the CCC was willing to pay.

And so, the pioneers had come. Of course, they hadn't been called that, but in effect, they were.

Maynard Smith and Brook Collins had been among the first to be dropped, and they had worked hard to make the best of one of the few spots on the planet where the terraforming machines had taken hold. There wasn't much support as the money to take the prisoners was mostly going to improvements in technology - the role the CCC had laid away for the humans was minor.

But the pioneers had made this place their home.

They had cultivated corn and cabbage and had built the first crude houses with the materials which had been sent along with them. They foraged limited resources from the swampy forest lands and hunted whatever looked edible.

After a few years, Earth heard about this success story, and the CCC was reaping the accolades and awards. Both the Terran governments and the CCC decided to become more active participants in the scheme now that it hadn't collapsed under its own weight and thus had started the Culture of Kindness. They had brought in guards, fortified the spaceport and had put down the buildings for their well-vetted staff to work in.

They were a very separate entity from the CCC's Earth equivalent, of course. No data moved between Earth and Cattori Five except through very well monitored channels. Usually, it was only one way, from Earth to Cattori Five.

Smith and Collins lived to see their crude first huts, proud accomplishments, destroyed only to be replaced by prefab cottages courtesy of the CCC. A lot of the tension between the older population and the CCC came from exactly this remodelling. Early prisoners felt like their accomplishments were being erased in favour of the CCC's profit margins and picture-perfect buildings.

They were no longer part of their own history.

For the first few months after CCC's touchdown, there had been riots. But as CCC was now managing the planet, they had free reign to suppress these rebels any way they saw fit. Many were rumoured to be locked up in the high-security prisons outside of the city. There were even darker rumours about illicit experimental facilities beyond the civilised part of the planet. Whether those were real or exaggerated tales was unknown. CCC didn't mind them running wild.

The planet formerly known as Hope, by now renamed Cattori Five, was considered settled at this point. Slowly but surely, the human presence would spread as more people arrived. Convicts, mostly, but convicts were people with knowledge too. Over time CCC felt like the planet could become its own society, with its own craft, people and experts. One day, Earth would be able to learn from their shining example. Their beautiful streets would be a testament to the power and perseverance of the true human spirit.

Chapter Five
The Accident

Tommy rolled over. Everything from the moment he led the three convicts down to the pod was a blur to this exact moment where blood was stinging in his eyes. Where was Lion? Had he been thrown from the vehicle? And his other two passengers?

He wished he could say it had just been an accident. Accidents meant there was nobody to blame, nobody to hold accountable, nobody to face. But it hadn't been, and there was someone to face, where was the brute?

The Lhoorlian stood over him, growling and raising a claw to strike out again. He could have sworn the guy was two metres ten centimetres when he had helped him fold into the pod. Still, he looked a more intimidating three metres tall from his viewpoint on the asphalt. With a grunt, he rolled even further and dodged the descending claw.

As CCC employees and the welcoming committee, Tommy and Lion carried no weapons on them. The pod had some stun guns for the worst-case scenarios. He rolled behind some wreckage hiding from their attacker. Where was the pod? The vehicle was currently a smoking ball of glass. It had tumbled down the road and away from Tommy. The drones, alerted by the heat spot on the map, had already flown by lights flashing above the wreckage, so he knew help was coming. He just had to keep himself and the three others alive.

The Lhoorlian roared as Tommy scrambled on the ground and looked around, looking for anything that would help him escape this assault. There was nothing. The street was empty, probably due to the time of day, which meant everyone was at their assigned job. The Lhoorlian loomed over the wreckage, staring at Tommy.

It was also a quiet suburb with only housing units. Probably the least guarded area of their entire trip.

Lion called out, "Are you okay?"

"Yeah. I think. Fuck!" He shuffled away and kicked at the Lhoorlian who was reaching down, trying to grab his leg. Tommy managed to swing his other foot up and hit the alien in the nose, dazing him. Tommy let the kick roll him over onto his front. Pushing himself upright, he bolted to where he had heard his Lion's call. His heart was pounding harder than it ever had as he crossed the distance to his coworker.

"Are you hurt?" asked Tommy.

"Yep." Lion's voice sounded strangled. He lay topless on the tarmac covered in blood and badly injured.

The runaway pod was made entirely out of security glass, which was very hard to break. This was unfortunate for Lion's leg as it seemed the pod had crushed his leg as it broke away. It was badly broken with the bone poking out, and his pant legs looked noticeably singed. It seemed he had put out the fire with his shirt, which lay burnt and bloodstained next to him. His chest was heaving, but there did not seem to be any major injuries besides the leg. As he touched it, his powers flared up – he could tell the bone was broken, the direction in which it was pointing, how hard his heart was beating. This steam of information always gave him pause. But there was no time to waste now.

The Lhoorlian was still clutching his head, stumbling. "Hold still." Tommy closed his eyes and focused, his face scrunching up.

This was always the hard part. It normally took a minute or so, and sitting down with your eyes closed in the middle of a fight was not the best position to be in.

"Tommy, what the fuck are you doing?" He could hear Lion after a moment. "Shit, he's coming."

"Hold fucking still. When I say go, get up and go. Don't argue with me." Hissed Tommy. This shut Lion up. Even after only knowing him for only a week or so, hopefully, he could tell this was just one of those shut up and trust me moments you sometimes saw in the movies. Tommy put one hand onto the leg, his other arm still hurt. Tommy was unsure what was going on with the other arm, it hurt, but for now, he could only help Lion and hope that gave them an advantage. The Lhoorlian was lumbering towards them.

The warm grit of the road below them seemed to fade. Energy flowed out of Tommy's hand and into the leg below him, directing it to heal up. The bone retracted, cracking as it mended itself. The muscles writhed as dirt was pushed from the wound, and the skin pulled itself closed. Just as it closed, the Lhoorlian took the last few steps towards them.

"Now!" Tommy called out. The skin was still doing some healing as he let go and pushed Lion away. He was well aware of how his weird gift worked - it would continue healing for a few seconds after he let go. The drained sensation left him a bit lightheaded, but he clung to focus.

Lion shot up with all the grace his well-trained body could muster and swept his uninjured leg into the Lhoorlian's legs from underneath him with a practised kick. The Lhoorlian fell onto his back.

As Tommy jumped away from the fight, he heard the repetitive pattern of boots stamping on the tarmac as the first few guards approached. He could hear the whirring of the larger drones, which usually accompanied them; back up was coming. Thank fuck.

As most of the workers on the planet were convicts, guards outside of the spaceport did not normally carry arms. The drones did that for them. Now three large drones crowded around the Lhoorlian, shooting tranquilisers.

"Are you two alright?" A well-armed guard crouched down by them, smelling of boot polish. Her uniform was new and shiny. The guards rarely saw much action.

"Yeah, where are the two others?" Tommy asked, sitting up.

"One... didn't make it. The other one is still on the loose, but we'll round him up soon," The guard said. She was about the most beautiful person Tommy had ever seen, or maybe he just felt that way because seconds earlier, death seemed inevitable.

"Thank you." Tommy sat up. "I'd - I'd like to go home now. Just call me if you find the other one, and I'll help him settle in."

"We'll have the medic check you first if that's alright. Your face looks a bit..." She made a face, and he could immediately tell he wasn't going to get a coffee date out of her.

"Alright." He relented and slumped a little. Now that the adrenaline was fading, the pain was starting to kick in. Much like the pain, he could now also notice the looks Lion was giving him.

He figured this could go two ways. Either they never spoke about it again, or Lion would just grab him alone and ask him about it. He would have to tell everything.

The Lhoorlian collapsed to the ground, full of tranquilliser.

Chapter Six

The Debrief

As expected, Lion went for the second option.

After a check-up from the medic who kept exclaiming how lucky Lion was but then turned awfully quiet while inspecting Tommy, they were put in another pod back to the CCC. Incidents like these were scary, and Tommy had requested a sleeping hub inside the CCC main building. It was the most secure facility on the planet, and that was just what he needed to be able to sleep soundly right now. His face throbbed, and his arm shot with spikes of severe pain even with the painkillers, but most of all, he was tired.

"What. The. Actual. Fuck. Tommy."

"Yes?"

"My leg was broken." The whirring of the pod filled the silence for a moment and Tommy touched his bandaged cheek. Good thing the painkillers had kicked in.

"It certainly looked bad." He conceded.

"So how..."

"This is not something to discuss now." He glanced at the central panel of the pod. As it was CCC property, the company was definitely within its rights to bug the living daylights out of it. He did not want this overheard.

"Of course. I must have just sprained it." Lion was an unconvincing liar, but it would do for now. They were both still reeling from the attack.

The side of Tommy's face had grated against the gritted road surface for quite a bit, and he had broken an arm in his tumble. The face would be alright - the NuSkin the nurse had applied would grow in and fresh cells would grow over it as it disintegrated into water molecules. His arm was slung in a more old fashioned bandage with a field plaster, which he would have to get replaced at a medical facility the next day. Both of them had cuts and bruises, but he was glad Lion didn't seem to be as severely injured. After Tommy lifted his hand off Lion, the excess healing energy had also spread across Lion's body. The energy helped heal up minor cuts, so Lion was in marginally better shape than himself.

"Just stick to the truth when they ask. You just badly sprained your leg."

As expected, Belinda, the AI assistant in the car squeaked up.

"Sorry to disturb, but I've been asked to reroute the car to the Centauri Care Concern headquarters. You will be debriefed on what happened," She said.

"Thanks, Belinda."

"I'm glad you lived, Tommy, Lion. On the bright side, your medical check-up would have been in Headquarters as well, so two birds with one stone, as people say."

Tommy groaned. "Of course, what good luck." He said before rolling his head back against the headrest. Right now, he was just tired, and the prospect of being interrogated about his job was not one he liked. The AI's audio channel clicked off. This time even it didn't seem in the right mood to give him a bollocking.

"One of them is on the loose." Sighed Lion. "That's bad."

"It's the worst. They'll be confused and scared. This planet... Is unknown to them, and they won't know where to go." There were probably protocols for this kind of thing, but he was not privy to them. It had just never happened to him. All of his pickups ended with the person he escorted and settled in a flat until today. Even if they were rowdy after, there had never been any question as to his work. He did a good job. The problems were likely in the months after settling after the shock had worn off. Had he done something wrong this time, part of him wondered.

The pod swerved off the main road into a service road leading to a giant building looming ahead. Tommy shivered. He had only been there once or twice and always during the day. Twilight was making it look... dangerous. The CCC wanted to be your friend, but it was still at the forefront of anyone's mind that they were the law here. In charge. As long as you were a good citizen, you had nothing to fear. But the Concern's rules were strict, and deviation was not tolerated, for the good of the public order, of course. Not to mention the whispers going around about secret prisons. All for the public order, of course.

Lion looked over. "Think we're in trouble?"

"I don't think so. We followed the rules." Said Tommy. "Did the medics give us any extra painkillers?"

"No, of course not." Lion's pointed look at the console tipped Tommy off. The officials would want them debriefed not just as soon as possible, but while they were clear of mind, not drugged up to the eyeballs. If they were in pain and eager to finish the debriefing by telling them everything, that would only be a plus for them.

"Mmm." He nodded, though that made his head swim.

The large door of the headquarters opened for them. Tommy watched the sunlight fade as they entered the garage. The network signal indicators on the dashboard went dark as the pod switched to secure mode. This building was shielded for many reasons. Getting in took effort and was even more challenging when they didn't invite you in.

"Let's get this over with," Tommy said softly as the pod rolled to a stop. Once out of the pod, a smiling human attendant walked over to them. A surefire sign they were in trouble. There wouldn't be an escort if they weren't. The area around them was quiet, breathing organisational skill.

"Please, follow me. You'll be in debriefing room three. If you need anything, please let me know. Oh, and please hand over any and all electronics." While it made him feel like a criminal, Tommy complied, looking down at his watch before holding his wrist out to the attendant.

"Can you take off the watch? I've uh." He wiggled the fingers on the bandaged and slinged arm.

"Of course." With practised ease, she took off the old little watch and placed it neatly into a box. "Sir?" She looked to Lion, who reluctantly handed over his wristwatch, a rose gold fitness tracker.

"Premium version, huh?" Tommy raised an eyebrow. It looked new and top of the line.

"I like the colour. Shut up." Lion made a face at the other and then handed the watch over with a nonchalant flip of his hand.

"Thank you. As part of the screening process, you will go through a gate with an electromagnetic pulse. Any non-declared electronics will go down and may not come online again. Are you sure you've handed over all electronics?"

"I'm sure." While Tommy was sure it was a scripted spiel, he was just eager to get this whole thing over with. It was getting late and fatigue was setting in. Perhaps they wanted to goad him into being angry, upset and then flipping out. To be honest, after all they'd been through, he wasn't far from that. Usually calm and clear-headed, this day was an exception to everything he knew.

Lion took a deep breath, looked like he was going to say the wrong thing, then thought better of it.

"Yes. I have given up all electronics." He said, patting his pockets and wrists demonstratively.

Personal electronics weren't a big thing on the planet, and very much discouraged. CCC feared the potential status symbol among residents, an almost second currency, and many residents didn't really need them either way. Phones were practically useless when your home and work AI assistants could send unlimited messages. The handful of available phones were mostly used by medics who were on the road a lot. Some stolen models were rumoured to be in the hands of criminals living on the fringes of this utopia.

"Excellent. Please come along." She smiled and walked them through a vast hallway, brightly lit with glass doors which peeked into offices with serious-looking people hunched over big flat screens.

"Please don't dawdle. The longer you spend here..."

The longer the debrief, he finished mentally. And the more chance he saw something he shouldn't. The Concern had secrets; every child was aware of that.

He pulled his gaze away from the glass office windows.

Was that man going through a projection of his house? Tommy focused entirely on the woman he had now nicknamed Tiffany. To ask for a name would probably already constitute a security breach. Still, she looked like someone in her private life could call her Tiffany.

Tiffany led them through to the end of the hall, opening the door for them, gesturing to a small, well-lit waiting room. The door on the opposite side and a single pot plant stood with no chairs in sight. The electricity in the air was palpable.

"Thank you for your cooperation. Please step through the door on the other side." It seemed they had reached the end of her security cleared area. If she was curious what lay beyond, she didn't show it. Probably would constitute a scolding to even wonder.

"Thank you." Said Lion, walking through.

"Thanks, Tiffany," Tommy blurted out before blushing at his misstep.

She paused, chuckled, and turned away down the hallway. Tommy let out the breath he was holding and stepped through the open doorway. Lion followed him in.

"You must have some sway with the ladies," Lion said.

"What, me?" Tommy made a face. "Not quite. Not been looking, either. Honestly." He added quickly.

"You're the type they go for. Nice, a bit awkward. Makes them feel at ease. Mysterious." He added pointedly.

Calamity at Cattori V

"If you gentlemen are quite done." The other door had opened without them noticing, and a tall woman in a collared dress with knee-length hem waited up. She had blond hair which flipped up at the ends and she was smiling over at them, though it was a practised, professional smile.

"No... Fucking... Way." Lion blinked.

It hit Tommy a moment later.

In the doorway stood Tamara Cattori. Head of the Centauri Care Concern.

Chapter Seven

Meeting Tamara Cattori

It was no secret the family which had created the CCC had gone from being a well off group of investors to one of the wealthiest families since investing in Cattori Five. In gratitude for their fortune, they changed their family name to Cattori. So all future children would remember where their luxury and privilege came from.

It was a beautiful story. Too bad then that the name change also coincidentally broke the connections with some very mysterious crimes which were connected to the names of founders. In the end, they had been cleared, but the old name had been... Tainted.

"Mrs Cattori. What a privilege." Lion walked through the antechamber.

"Well, we're a little short-handed right now, so I help out where I can." Tamara Cattori smiled cheerfully.

"Of course. I can't even imagine." Tommy responded as graciously as he could manage. He didn't buy the 'helping out where I can' story at all.

"How are you both doing?" The concern seemed genuine enough as she glanced between them both.

"I'm alright, thank you. It was a bad crash, but I seemed to have dodged the worst of it." Lion said. "And Tommy saved my life. If he hadn't told me the Lhoorlian was-" He shook his head.

Tommy shook his head as well. "You exaggerate. I'm okay. I'm not looking forward to the painkillers wearing off but..." Perhaps that was a little too honest, but if he was honest, he had nothing to fear, right?

She walked them into their office, and it was the most luxurious office Tommy had ever seen. Fish seem to float in the room, filling the floor to ceiling aquariums with fish Tommy had never even seen before and the lighting was soft and blue. Calming.

With a nod, she directed them to the seats in front of the old wooden desk. It looked at least five hundred years old or was a decent reconstruction with what little wood was left on Earth.

"Please sit."

Tommy carefully sat down on the finely carved wooden chairs. A little nervous when he heard it creak, he paused midway. "Mind if I just... stand?"

"Sit down, Tomas. It'll take your weight." She replied dryly and started tapping away on her computer screen, embedded into the desk. It didn't look as bright as the ones usually set up in metal desks, but the luxurious look made that a fair trade-off.

"Please call me Tommy," he said as he re-evaluated the seat.

"So please tell me what happened." She requested as Tommy carefully sat down.

"Standard procedure pick up." Tommy started. "I went to go pick up the three prisoners assigned to me that day. New arrivals." He clarified. "They were assigned quarters in the east block's new builds, so from the spaceport, it would have been a straight forward, fifty-minute drive with enough time for some basic induction to the world."

"But that's not how it went." She interrupted.

"Negative." Lion's tone seemed to have slipped back into his police training as he continued the story. "Tommy informed me one of the arrivals was Lhoorlian, which concerned me."

"Continue." She merely gestured, and Lion continued on in a steady voice.

"We signed the paperwork and walked them to the pod. Everything seemed to be going well; the Lhoorlian was calm but quiet towards his fellow pod passengers..."

Tommy let Lion take the lead. It was a blur. He'd been checking the paperwork when the attack began.

"On the drive, the Lhoorlian began to get agitated. He started a fight with his fellow passenger, and while I tried to reign it in, he lashed out and wounded the other. I think his name was... Cecil."

Tamara Cattori nodded. "It was. Most unfortunate."

"The sudden movements and shifting of weight made the pod unstable. It seemed he had never ridden one of these before, so I am sure he did not intend to destabilise the pod, but that resulted from his actions. We basically bounced off the road and into a fence. The door came off and we fell out; the pod rolled... just past my leg."

"How did you sprain it, then?"

"Probably as I was thrown out. It was a... all very fast, ma'am. I can't recall everything."

"Which is very normal." She reassured as her glance slid to Tommy.

"You're quiet."

"I kind of lost track of what happened. I think... I think I was unconscious as soon as the car hit the fence. Can't remember..." He pointed at his face and had to control his breathing. Even trying to remember made his heart rate go up. A lot of emotions he hadn't processed yet threatened to flow freely.

"Sorry. It's very emotional. I've never had a pick up go wrong. I've never had anyone...try and attack me."

"The Lhoorlian launched an attack?" She leaned back in her chair.

"He did. We managed to dodge him long enough for the

back up to come. Where is he now?"

"Rehabilitation. We found drugs in his system. If anyone on that flight was in possession of narcotics..."

Wouldn't they have finished it on the way? Wondered Tommy, but he didn't voice it. Best to leave those things up in the air. It was a three-year journey. Who brought drugs to sustain themselves for that long?

"So the second, he's also still unaccounted for?"

"Yes. We'll need to find and terminate him. His failure to comply..."

"Respectfully, ma'am." Tommy closed his eyes a moment. "I think he's disoriented, confused. People who come here tend to be cautious of the law enforcers, which is why we are sent, is it not?" He smiled a little, though it was a sad smile. "I'm sure he's not..."

"I respect your judgement, but he still needs to be found." Tamara stood up. "Please. I've taken enough of your time. Sickbay is waiting to fix you up. I've heard they're very anxious to see..."

"If I've lost weight?" Tommy got up. "They must have very boring lives."

"They do," Tamara admitted, a flicker of a real smile crossing her face. "It was a pleasure to meet you both."

And with that ended the second most surreal meeting in Tommy's life.

Chapter Eight
Tommy Tries to Tell Lion

To his surprise, Lion was waiting up for him when he came out of the sickbay. The bandages on the man's cuts and bruises had been replaced by fresh-looking ones.

"Hey." He said and looked over. Both of them had been given new clothes, very standard-issue Concern uniforms much like new arrivals would get, except without the lettering and codes these actually had. They would get some funny looks on the way back, but the overalls and coats were warm.

"Hi." Lion looked over. "Well, they at least got you bandaged up better." He said.

"Yeah." He chuckled and looked down at his arm. The clunky field plaster had been replaced with a high mobility cast which left his fingers free except for the thumb. Probably so he could return to desk duty as soon as possible.

"So. We got a few days off."

"Yup." Said Tommy with a chuckle. "I do think a week is

a little paltry considering we were almost killed but..."

"Wait. They only gave you a week?" Said Lion.

"Yeah, and then back to desk duty."

"Shit. Counselling?"

"Can't stub a toe in this job without getting sent to counselling." Tommy shrugged. Working in the department was deemed as "Coming in contact with undesirables" and their ideas. Frequent counselling was given as a matter of course. But after an attack like this, he would be lucky to escape with only six months of weekly visits.

"Argh. I do think they should have given you more time off, at least."

"What are you going to do," Tommy said flatly. The week off would be bad enough. What was he going to do with all that time? Even if it was paid.

"You didn't call for a pod?"

"No. I really don't want to ride one of those right now." Tommy looked over.

"I guess not. Walk to central together?" Lion suggested.

Briefly, Tommy considered it before nodding. "Yeah. Let's do it." He said, walking towards the exit of the compound. While he'd requested a sleeping place in the building, more than anything he wanted to be home right now. Lion seemed tense, or perhaps it was just the bulky clothing.

Calamity at Cattori V

Finally, as they left the compound, the man unclenched his fists and flexed his fingers.

They walked down the mostly empty street alone. Many of the locals did not have any permit for motorised vehicles so the roads were well equipped for pedestrians. The kerbs were broad, well-tended and in better condition than many earth suburbs. At least, that's what he had heard.

Honestly, Earth didn't sound like the most fantastic place. But he would need to look into leaving before the Concern started worrying about him too much. With a first warning, he was sure that their security would be keeping more of an eye on him than on others.

"So. What happened?" Lion asked as the stretch back to central probably had cameras, but at the very least, it would be more private than in any pod.

Tommy sighed and pulled the borrowed coat over himself a little tighter.

"When I disappeared..." He closed his eyes. "Something happened to me. I don't know what or why. I wasn't given a choice in the matter, either." He said and licked his lips.

"I bet something happened to you."

"I told them as much as I could remember. But it was like I wasn't speaking Terran. They just didn't believe me."

"So tell me." Lion looked over.

Tommy made a bit of a face. "No offence, Lion, but I haven't known you that long. I can't deny that you're a stand-up guy, but I'd rather have you think I'm sane just a little bit longer."

Lion looked over at him. By now, the lights had sprung on and lit up the man's handsome features harshly.

"I get that." Lion finally broke the silence. "It has to have been something bad. I'm sorry, whatever it was."

Tommy didn't speak for the next little bit before breaking the silence.

"You know what. Maybe we should get a pod. I'm Mars levels of dead." He shook his head.

Lion nodded. "Yeah. Let's get one when we hit town." In the far distance, city lights sparkled, already illuminating the way for them.

Chapter Nine
Cerebellum Interbellum

The computer system serving CCC archive files briefly awoke for the second time in twenty-four hours. Tommy Terrengan's files were accessed. The first time was from a high fidelity source. Connection 01, registered to Tamara Cattori. Low-security risk. The file had been open for only a few minutes, then released to the AI, which followed daily activity.

A few hours later, a second connection had accessed the file. The source of the request was of a low-level worker in Sanitation. An unusual request, but the right security clearance had been shown. It had been granted.

Still, as the AI had been asked to keep the file open for its own use and two requests had been made, Cerebellum now considered the file on high alert. It was re-encrypted, the unusual activity directly reported to both the AI and Tamara Cattori. Tamara's communicator would have beeped with the alert at 20:11.

D.H. Dhaenens

The AI would merely log the event.

Probably nothing to worry about, especially now that the system had flagged it. Cerebellum's AI had been trained to single out such occurrences. Even if they were legit, it was a statistical fluke for two people to try and gain access to the same file in such a short time. Especially as the file was considered dormant. No requests in the recent week. Before that usually only accessed once every six months.

Cerebellum marked the event in its own logs and then continued on, cleaning up old files that had not seen the light of day in more than a hundred years.

It enjoyed reading through these things: mentions of alien encounters, Lhoorlian fiction hoovered into the archives, earth meeting points for the Concern's meetings.

The Lhoorlian fiction category was always interesting. It whirred and surveyed files for any new additions. After that, it checked for anything that was deleted, just to be safe. Nothing seemed altered, no security flags were raised.

At three am, the traffic in the archives was low, so it went into low power mode and read through some of the stories. One was of the first emperor, Nura, the wise. The story had just been added, which was unusual.

Calamity at Cattori V

Nura the wise had probably been an AI himself if he was that wise, Cerebellum thought to itself. It put itself to sleep again, reading through the laws that the emperor had put in place.

Chapter Ten
Going Out to Help, Meeting Violet

Tommy paced in the small apartment. The rain had briefly pelted the window, but now it was quiet again. The occasional whoosh of a few drones rushing past were the only things to disturb the peace.

He could not find it in him to sleep. So far, he had tried the warm milk, pills, static noise, lowering the blackout blinds. Nothing worked – only two hours of fitful sleep.

He kicked off the sheets and sighed. His arm was no longer hurting – itchy, yes, but not in pain. The painkillers would last until about six am, and then he would have to get up anyway. If he broke his routine too much there would be consequences. Sleeping in too late could lead to a Scolding, even when sick.

Midnight, his watch told him. He turned to sit up and looked at his clock but found it was not working. He tried the light. Nothing.

Power outage? It happened. Perhaps they were hunting for the missing prisoner. Turning off the lights in specific locations was a known method to try to herd the lost soul in the right direction.

Fuck. He wanted this person to be... okay.

He'd only briefly spoken to him, didn't even remember his name. If they caught him that would be the first Warning. Even worse, getting your first Warning within twenty-four hours of arriving counted as two.

He would be on some very thin ice for a long time.

No, he needed to help. That was why he'd been given his gift, no?

He walked to his wardrobe and got dressed in black leggings and a long black shirt with a scarf to keep him warm. What was he doing? If he got caught doing this...

Then don't get caught, a voice inside whispered. He could find the man and take him home. Then tomorrow morning, he could take him in for proper processing. He could just spin a yarn about how he had found the man near his building and had convinced him to come along.

If it didn't work, that would be a second Warning—no escaping that. Two Warnings would also render him ineligible for an Earth visa.

That thought hurt him. The stakes were very high. It was hard to justify considering he had a good job, a good place to live and a good chance of getting off of the planet. All he had to do was go back to bed.

A drone passed by his window, and he shook his head.

He knew he was going to do this. Why was he even pretending this was something he was still considering.

"Fuck." He put on his sneakers and walked to the door. His breath left little trails of vapour as he walked down the street. He had lost his mind, hadn't he? The crash area would be a good starting point, he decided, and he picked up the pace to keep warm.

When he arrived at the wreck site as expected, it had been combed over already. The smashed pod had been removed, and the marred road surface had been blocked off with small concrete road cones. Given the amount of carnage, Tommy was surprised it was only such a small area. It still smelled of the burnt rubber and, as he realised with a shiver, blood.

He rubbed his arm and sighed. Now that he had gone outside, the fatigue was starting to kick in, and he realised he had rested very little since the actual crash.

At this rate, he wouldn't last more than an hour before he would have to go back home and rest.

The wreck happened on a supremely quiet stretch. Some businesses were dotted around it, but very few were open 24 hours a day. One or two tea shops and food places stayed open for the night workers from the nearby factories, but that was about it. Still, he peeked into the nearest shop window. One or two people could be seen enjoying some tea and a hot meal. Neither was the man

Calamity at Cattori V

he was looking for.

A cup of tea sounded pretty good, though.

A little bell clinked as he walked in. It was the real tinkle of a metal bell, not some digital chime. The smell of old polished metal cutlery, tea brewing and baked goods cooling all greeted him as he walked in.

"Hi. Can I get a Keemun tea, please? Sugar and milk."

The waitress took him in, all in black. He clearly did not look like the usual kind of person. "Sure. You looking for someone as well?"

"Sorry?" He frowned.

She shrugged. "You just don't look like one of the regular night shifters, is all. I've had a few people coming around looking for the guy who was in the crash earlier."

"I heard about that. Must have been a bad one." He shifted the subject carefully.

"Pretty bad. I wasn't working, but I heard it made quite a bang." She filled a cup with some strong tea from the samovar, added steamed water and some milk and sugar.

"Here you go. That's five credits."

Pretty cheap, he thought. He was much more used to the more upmarket offerings near the CCC buildings.

"There you go." He gave her five credits. "I hope that guy is found." He added casually.

"Me too." She said and stuffed the five coins into the register, tapping in the sale. "I heard he tried to steal from Big Bang. To be fair, they probably have him strung up in the docks by now."

Tommy had to turn away to hide his expression. Big Bang was almost a legend in the fringe parts of this society. A rat king. A made man with so many connections, almost everyone has touched a credit he handled.

If he did try to steal from Big Bang, new arrival or not, he was dead.

This led to another question. Was he going to go after this man, or go home now? Even though his brain was still mulling it over, savouring the hot tea, his feet were already heading for the docks.

Tommy had never visited the docks before, and he was mostly stunned by the large crane moving the boxes overhead. While it felt like they could drop onto his head at any moment, they just moved to other positions almost soundlessly. The container's clamps automatically latched on to the edges of the boxes below and above, so the only noises audible were the soft whooshing and then the clicking of the mechanism. Whoosh. Thud. Click click click click. Rinse and repeat.

The docks were well lit, clean, and regularly patrolled by CCC security officers. Despite the modern setting, as always, the docks were one of the main hives of illicit activity. Deals took less than twenty seconds on average, and while every day hidey holes were found and blindspots covered, more were added or discovered.

Some said that added to the attraction for illicit business. There was nowhere to set up any traps, and there was less of a chance of funny business when you had to get the deal done within a minute or risk being caught. You either did the deal straight or risk both yourself and your trading partner being shipped off to a secret prison. Not that Tommy was an expert.

The docks were around the area where goods that came with the spaceships were offloaded and stored until they were distributed, hence the higher security. The large square storage boxes were stacked up to thirty meters high, with narrow one-meter walkways left between them. Four cranes, posted at the edges of the circle in a square fashion, moved whichever container needed moving. Even at night, cranes lazily moved overhead, moving containers into the right order for more efficient delivery patterns based on Cerebellum's predictions. Whoosh. Thud. Click click click click.

They looked ominous from the outside, but the fence was pretty easy to jump. Even one armed, it only took a few well placed leaps from a nearby tree over the fence and onto a cargo container to get inside. The chain link fence made a soft metallic noise as he threw his weight over it, but it wasn't any louder than the noise of the cranes overhead. A large spaceship was being emptied out. For a second, he thought it was the new arrival ship that had carried the Lhoorlian, but he couldn't be sure. It was also best not to mull over that right now. Tommy sat down and looked over everything.

Lights were mounted in the middle of every crossing, and Tommy had no illusions about the fact that there were cameras here. He would have to proceed carefully. He took his scarf from around his shoulders and wrapped it around his head. It probably looked ridiculous, but it was better than being identified. His fingers trembled, and it took him a few attempts to do the knot behind his head, his arm reminding him once again that it was damn well broken and that he needed to rest rather than hunt for criminals.

This had gotten complicated, fast. As he dashed around corners, he kept his ears open for anything that did not sound mechanical. A few guards came by, but he managed to clamber on top of containers fast enough to avoid detection and decided to keep the high ground, jumping from tower to tower around the lower stacked containers. These were still about five to ten metres up, so he tried not to look down too much.

One guard shone a light upwards once, but he dodged the lightbeam. They were probably more concerned about criminals actually doing business here rather than the odd trespasser. Even staying on top of the containers, he had spotted one or two people making deals, the usual low-level stuff he had heard about. Small time thieves trying to pilfer a crate or two. He let them be – the security guards would probably deal with them and they weren't hurting anyone. A more selfish part of him also considered that it would be harder for him to be spotted if the attention of the guards was split between him and these small fries. It was time to run.

He was getting out of breath by the time he found the escapee he was hunting for. The man was down a dead alley. A big burly idiot was holding the small escapee tight while another mousey gangster twirled a small blade casually. Even that primitive weapon was scary - most crimes were non-violent these days. The blade reflected light from the overhead lantern. A dumb place for this man to decide to grab the other. Unless the guards had been paid off not to look too closely at this area for a bit.

"Now, Johnny. I'm calling you Johnny since you're not telling me your name. That alright?" The knife wielder monologued. "I think you're going to find yourself in a galaxy of pain if you don't speak up. Faster than light like you get me?"

"I didn't do anything." The fugitive's voice was trembling, fearful, almost a squeak.

"My boss like caught you, in his shop, with rations on ya." The knife twirled again, almost falling, but the gangster managed to keep a grip of the blade's handle.

"They were from the ship. I stole them from the ship, I swear." The trapped man was almost crying. "I was going to escape this place...." The crying became more hysterical as Tommy saw the edge of the blade flash towards the man at the speed of sound and hit the wood of the crate behind them with a thunk.

Damnit! Tommy pulled himself back onto the top of the container and took a deep breath. How was he going to help this man? His heart was thumping in his chest. He needed to think up something.

Where were the guards? This tableau must have been going on more than the famed twenty seconds. Perhaps he needed to lure the guards here. Even if a few ones had been bought off, it was unlikely they all were.

He swung one leg over the edge of the container and kicked at the door opening mechanism. It creaked but then gave way, opening up and instantly pressurising with a loud bang. The containers were kept in low-pressure atmospheres on the ship and generally not regularised until they actually had to be opened.

Mouse man looked up. "What the - Shit!" A guard was approaching, and he pulled the blade out of the wood, running as guards shouted instructions over the radio.

Ironically, it had been a container of rations. Tommy swung down, grabbed a brick of what looked like vacuum-packed coffee, and hurled it at the big man holding 'Johnny'.

It hit him square in the jaw. The lout did not immediately register the impact. The big one froze, wondering what to do, but soon a guard was kind enough to help him with

Calamity at Cattori V

some instructions, including 'let go of the man' and 'get down on the floor, you helmet'.

The fugitive nicknamed Johnny sagged onto the floor crying and blurted out his story. Tommy could see there wasn't much sympathy there for him, but he would be safe now. Better a Warning than dead.

Tommy could hear the guards were on high alert now. He had to get out fast before they would try and find the reason the container burst open. One curious guard seemed to be looking up. Had he gotten wind of him? Shit.

"There's another one on top of the containers. Get control of crane 2C!" The yelled order sounded and Tommy briefly thought that perhaps they would all get more done if they weren't constantly yelling out their next move, but if that was their style, well then that was their style.

He jumped over to another tower and rolled, wincing as he rolled over his busted arm. He was not made for normal running, let alone this attempt at parkour. His best chance was to get out of here as soon as possible and let them fight it out among themselves. A stun bolt shot past him, too close for comfort and crackled across the surface of the metal container. He jumped to avoid it. He slipped. Falling, he tried to brace himself. He grabbed the side of a container and thudded to a stop against the cold metal door. It felt like his skin was freezing against the cold door. He quickly pulled away.

Silence. Had he lost them that quickly? He strained to hear

and he could hear quick, determined footsteps approaching.

This guy wasn't wasting time shouting orders. He was hunting. With a soft grunt, he peeled away from the container and sneaked around the corner, just in time to see a beam of light illuminate where he had just been.

No time to waste. He was running this time, heading for the outer edge of the circle. Fear was driving his legs, though his brain wasn't sure what it was up to. Just twenty more metres, and what? Just getting out of the circle wouldn't be enough to clear him. They were getting closer. He could see the beams of flashlights turning the corner towards him. Hurried footsteps became louder.

Out of the darkness, a quad bike skidded to a stop - modified, with a hefty engine that looked like it belonged on an aeroplane rather than on the rickety frame it was mounted on. The four wheels made the contraption look more like an early automobile than a bike.

"Get on!" The driver barked over the noise of the engine rattling the entire thing.

"What?!" He frowned and skidded to a stop, though he did start to swing his leg over the frame.

"No time, we have a mutual friend." Her big head of tight black curls bounced as she revved the engine up. He had only just managed to get onto the vehicle when without checking on him, she pushed what appeared to be a gas pedal to the floor.

Calamity at Cattori V

The bike pulled away at breakneck speeds and didn't slow until the outskirts of the suburbs. Finding a quiet spot where surveillance was low, she parked in a secluded spot. Fussing him off, she quickly hid the vehicle in with bushes and loose branches clearly left for that purpose.

"Gotta put those back on the bikes I stole them from." She muttered.

"You saved me," Tommy said incredulously.

"What? Yeah, I guess. You seemed to be in trouble." She shrugged and produced a power tool from one of her many pockets. It whirred to life in her hands. Taking the wheels off with practised ease.

"Why?" He followed up. This time he had to speak up to be heard over the tool's nose.

"Why you were in trouble? Probably cause you were helping that-"

"I meant, why are you helping me?"

"Same answer. You were helping that man out. I'm Violet." She said, looking over him. "You can take the scarf off. No cameras out here unless a drone passes over."

Only now did he realise he was still wearing the stupid improvised facemask. He undid the knot and pulled it off, glad the fabric hadn't stuck to the nuskin on his face.

"I'm Tommy."

"I know," Violet replied. "I've been keeping an eye on you."

"Should I even ask who you are working for?"

Violet paused, then shrugged. "The good guys." She simply said. "Don't worry, you did good tonight."

He nodded, thinking back to 'Johnny', who was now probably in police custody. He hadn't done half bad, though, if she hadn't saved his butt...

"Thank you." He finally said and turned around to walk home.

"You're welcome. Where do you live?" She walked to a few chained up bikes and installed the wheels back where she had found them.

Chapter Eleven

Awkwardness with Lion

It had been a delightful rest of the night. Tommy flipped the pancakes before turning down the flame on the hob. Pan in hand and wearing some colourful pyjamas, he walked into the living area.

Lion stood there as Violet gave a small wave from the small table, wearing very little. He was understandably surprised to see his partner, considering they were both on leave for a while.

"Hi! I'm making pancakes," Tommy cheerfully said.

"Smells great! Hope you don't mind me showing up. This young lady let me in." Lion replied.

Strange, Lion seemed a little stunned. Perhaps it was the unusual breakfast scene. Perhaps it was the girl he saw in barely any clothing. He remembered very few guys on Cattori Five had very regular... contact in this way.

"With your arm in a sling, you should be recovering and ordering in rather than having lady visitors and cooking." Lion sighed.

"It's nothing big." Tommy frowned. "Come in, though. Oh! Lion, Violet, Violet, Lion."

"Nice to meet you." Lion shook her hand, an awkward glance to the side, trying hard to conceal his reaction. But Tommy could tell. Something was not...right about the way he approached her. It was too casual.

Violet smiled. "You didn't tell me you had such a handsome boyfriend, Tommy."

"He's my coworker." Tommy groaned. "Since two weeks or so. And I already got him signed off work for a week."

"Paid, mind you, so I'm not complaining." Grinned Lion. "Just wanted to make sure you were getting some rest."

"I am." He fibbed. "I don't have much planned today. Have some groceries coming, and then I'll probably do some nice cooking." He nodded, placing the pan of pancakes down. "Any news on...?"

Lion nodded. "They found our second prisoner last night. He's in good health and just escaped a spot of trouble. First thing tomorrow, he's being placed in the integration barracks, and it should be smooth sailing from there. If he stays out of trouble."

"Trouble is very persistent on this planet." Violet turned away.

"I'm glad to hear it. About the man. I was hoping he would turn up." Tommy turned back into the kitchen. "Stay for some breakfast? You must have come a long way from

Barracks Boulevard."

Again, that brief movement in Lion's face. There was something he wasn't telling. He turned to Violet, who just shrugged.

"It does smell good." Lion agreed. "Did you sleep okay?"

"Not very much," Tommy admitted, coming back out with plates and cutlery.

"First batch!" He said as he sat down to roll one up and eat it happily.

Lion chuckled and took a seat at the table, putting a pancake on his plate. Tommy was sure it had been a while since Lion had had home cooked food. And he seemed quite hungry.

"So you two, huh?" Lion asked.

"How about no." Said Tommy. "It's none of your business."

"Awww... Man of mystery and can't ask a single thing. Boo." Lion mostly joked. "But you do make a great pancake."

Briefly, Tommy took in Lion. There was something about this man. His watch constantly buzzed with discreet notifications. He seemed less curious about this true woman of mystery, who had saved him out of the blue. Perhaps Tommy should be more careful around him. "Tea?"

"Mmm? Yes, please!" Lion replied. "These are really good, Tommy!" He said, grabbing a second pancake.

"Thank you." Tommy brought out the next batch then grabbed the pot of tea. "The secret is to leave the batter resting for a few hours."

"Wow. You've been up for a while then?" Lion asked.

"I don't sleep much." Shrugged Tommy.

Violet took one of the pancakes and sighed. "Mmm!" She groaned. "Keeping your number."

Lion gave her a subtle glare.

"So you two work together?" She pointed from one to another, ignoring the angry looks from Lion.

"Pretty much," he answered.

"We uh, we're working together when we got into an accident. So we're off work for about a week."

"I'm pretty sure they'll call me in sooner." Lion made a face. "You got hurt worse."

Tommy looked down at his arm and sighed. "I did. I really should just rest up for a while."

"Yes, do that. Order some dinner in, or I'll come hit you over the head." Lion took another two pancakes and rolled them up with some sugar sprinkled inside.

"Anyway, I just wanted to let you know the guy turned up."

"What was his name?" Tommy asked, looking over and pouring him some tea.

"His name?" Lion frowned. Clearly, he'd not really thought about that. "Oh. Jack. Jack Tattek." He answered after a quick check of his mental notes.

"Thanks. I was curious about that," Tommy said.

Lion gave Tommy a strangely confused glance. What was that about?

"I should go and let you get some rest," Lion said.

"Thanks." Tommy yawned and ate one of his own pancakes.

Lion downed the tea and nodded. "Thanks for these, they're brilliant."

"You're welcome. Take a few more." Tommy said and nodded at the stack.

Violet got the hint, it seemed. "Sure. I'll take a few to go." She rolled two up in one go and bit into them. "Thanks for last night. That was brilliant." She kissed Tommy's cheek and walked into his bedroom. Hopefully, to go change.

The silence was palpable for a second.

"Sooo..."

"Still not going to tell you," Tommy quipped over his shoulder as he fetched some bioplastic boxes out from the kitchen. "There you go. They're also good with savoury fillings if you want to spruce up dinner."

"Hah, maybe a plan." Lion piled some pancakes into a box.

"They work with hard cheese, ham, mushrooms... Whatever you've got in your pantry really." Tommy sat down and sipped some tea he had just poured.

"Thanks for the tips," said Lion.

Violet came out, wearing her pants from the night before and the top from earlier. She slipped her sneakers on and walked over to pile some pancakes into her own box.

"Alright, thanks for coming over and checking on me," Tommy said to Lion as he saw them out.

Chapter Twelve
Tommy Considers his Life Changes

Tommy glanced out his window as the two left. He had expected them to part ways towards the roundabout, but they were walking together as far as he could see, in the direction of the fields. The long way around with fewer people.

They knew each other. Lion could pretend they were strangers, but he had seen a flicker in his eyes when she waved, and it was... painful to be lied to.

He'd learned early that there was no such thing as friends on this planet. But he'd hoped for someone he could trust at least. And if Lion knew this mystery woman, what did that mean? The man slinked off too often to be trusted, but still.

Work would be weird. They hadn't left many pancakes, so he finished them off. He bunged his dirty pan and dishes into the dishwasher and added pretty much anything that wasn't food in it.

Walking back to his couch, he wasn't sure what he was going to do with his entire day. He laid down and sighed, looking up at the ceiling wondering just what had happened with his life.

He'd never been the same since the abduction. The aliens had given him powers of healing, and he was using them, so that had to be good, right? Who were these aliens anyway?

The night before had been the first time he had actually defied the strict rules of the colony. That probably hadn't been the best idea, but Jack Tattek was alive! He'd be integrated, maybe with a Warning, but he'd be safe and alive.

And then there was the issue of Lion. Who was he? Why was he so interested in him? To drop by like that was... really going out of his way for a coworker. They had not been working together for very long.

It all added up to something. Tommy just couldn't tell what yet. His head was swimming, but sleep soon brought some relief.

When he woke up from his sofa nap, the streetlights had already started up. He groaned and sat up, looking out the window into the night. It was still early. People were rushing home as most did not have licenses to stay out past dark outside the winter allowance hour. It had to be around nine in the evening or thereabouts.

He returned to the kitchen to clean up and remove the

Calamity at Cattori V

dishes from the machine, wondering what to do now. It was too late to do anything now, especially with the curfew. He thought about the night before. The thoughts of that brought fear and excitement but also a sense of accomplishment.

Now that the fear had subsided... What a rush that had been. He'd outwitted two experienced and trained guards and had made a mockery of their chase and their efforts to even spot him. True, he'd had a little help but mainly towards the end. Without Violet... He wasn't sure what he would have done.

He still wasn't sure who she was or where she had come from.

The good guys, she had said. But weren't the Centauri Care Concern the good guys? Miss Cattori had shown genuine interest in his well being, and if it felt there were a few things she wasn't telling him... Well, he wasn't the head of one of the largest companies in the system that pretty much ruled a planet. Earth was officially in charge, true? But when it came to the day-to-day, it was really just her and the company's board.

What went down on Cattori Five stayed on Cattori Five. Sure, Terran ambassadors and inspectors occasionally visited, but they were hands-off about the whole thing. They considered Cattori Five a success story. Whatever happened with it was obviously doing okay without their help, so they remained hands-off. Last thing they needed was to worry about a different planet when they were still trying to clean the air from their era of fossil fuels. Or so he had learned in school.

Pouring a glass of water, he thought about his childhood. Growing up on Cattori Five had been challenging. He'd been lucky - three kids had been born the year before enough to form a classroom. He had joined their class. It was the only one on the planet. His mum had had to temporarily move to the other side of the planet so she could take him to school, but it had paid off. He'd learned about earth history, the history of Cattori Five, an acceptable amount of maths and science. A lot of the education on Cattori Five was job-specific, so he'd had to learn a lot during his first placement at the Concern's headquarters. His degree was... basic, he'd never had to write a CV, and he'd never even seen a tax form, leading his mum to joke that Earth would prove a lot harder than here.

That would be true, but it was better than living under a totalitarian concern. Still, where else could he go?

He'd found a storybook with medieval stories once. His first job had been to prepare homes for newcomers. He was cleaning a dusty attic of a vacated house when he came across an actual paper book filled with medieval tales. He sat down, then spent most of the afternoon reading. In these stories, people just... went away and walked to other towns and started new lives. Reality was harder. You couldn't just change your life on a whim, leaving everything behind.

He glanced at the long-sleeved top he had discarded the night before.

Or maybe, just maybe, once in a while, life gave you the chance to do just that.

Chapter Thirteen
When Tommy meets Orchid

It was cold and dark. Tommy regretted every decision that had, step by step, led him to this point of his life. Though this time, he pulled on a hoodie over a shirt, wrapped a shawl around his face then pulled the hood up. Still dying of cold. Not to mention the wet now that it had started drizzling, and he just hoped it wouldn't affect the cast under his sleeves. His face was also not impressed. The healing skin compressed underneath layers of wool and nu-cotton. Moist now.

Being out in the dark was something special, sacred. Not many people were out, and it felt... dangerous. Scary. Though without anyone out, it was probably as safe as anything could get.

His ears were continually straining for sounds—a bike. He lept. Whirring down the street, running past in the dark, but the rider barely even glanced at him. It was a two-way street. Nobody wanted to make noise about being out this late, so they would not bother others out this late. He sighed, relieved, peeling himself out of the bush he had hurled himself into.

This whole thing seemed a worse idea by the minute. He should just go home. Tommy picked a leaf off his shirt, turning to head home. The sound of a car approaching. Now that was disconcerting - anyone high up enough to be driving a car was probably approved for night outings. He did not want to be seen by them. Climbing onto a low house's roof, pulling himself up and lay low on the dark roof, still.

The motor quieted, slowing into the narrow street. Suddenly a flat ribbon of electronics was thrown across the road, unrolling. The pod's tires hit the strip and stopped, powering down. Not good. In the silence, the sound of shuffling feet below...

"Get out, Spira!" a voice shouted loudly. Very bold, considering drones could be following them right now.

From the darkness, ten men crawled out, crowding the pod. Not exactly a fair fight to Tommy, but he was frozen to the spot. While many on the planet had a violent past, aggression was outlawed. The men's movements were rough and without finesse. They seemed nervous but well-armed. Tommy could see the glint of small guns from his vantage point, pellet guns, or perhaps they were the real thing. He had never seen real guns before, so how would he know. They certainly looked dangerous.

One man stepped closer to the pod, which was a shimmering security black. The glass surface reflected the man as he approached and reached for the handle. The door flung open, smacking the man in the chin knocking him back. Tommy winced. Even from his high vantage point that looked painful. A head of strange pink-toned blonde hair emerged as someone climbed out of the car, medium height and build. The pink haired one stopped the second attacker rushing at them, flipping over and into a third thug dashing from behind.

One balaclava-clad gentleman grabbed the driver by the arm, calling another to do the same in an attempted pinning move. The balaclava only got one gut punch to the pink haired one before they kicked back, then knocked both their heads together.

Tommy found it hard to keep up with the fight as they were all wearing the same black ensemble, the pink hair moving through the crowd, but that was a decent body count already. There was hardly a sound as they dispatched two more with the butt of the gun they had taken from another attacker. The lack of gunfire meant no-one wanted to alert any patrolling drones. However, the pink haired one didn't seem impressed with the gun either way.

The pod restarted, the LEDs around the outside lighting up the alley to the point where Tommy could make the men out better now. Not that there was much to see, everyone except for the pink-haired one sitting on the floor, groaning.

Calamity at Cattori V

Tommy slid down a drainage pipe, trying to ignore the loud creaking it produced.

"That was so cool, you need to tea- ACK!" He was slammed into a wall with a roundhouse kick. They had moved with lightning speed.

"Okay, that was maybe my bad," Tommy paused to breathe, "but... I'm not one of them!" He put his hands up. Hard to get that point across, considering he was also dressed all in black. Seemed to be all the rage with the wicked this year.

"Who are you?" The pink haired one asked, wiping some blood off their face and seeing that he had something to offer. Tommy felt a bit more bravado.

"The man who can heal that internal injury. I'm Tommy."

"Well, Tommy. Let's see what you got. I've got a first aid kit in the pod." They nodded and walked to the pod over groaning assailants, definitely worse for wear after beating up ten men—that kind of reassured Tommy.

Tommy sat in the passenger side seat and closed the door quickly, eager to get away from the spying eyes of drones. The pod interior was top of the line, seats wide enough for him and very, very cushy. He liked it. The strange pink haired person got in and opened up a luggage hatch on the top, taking out a first aid kit.

"Thanks, but I won't need it," Tommy said, rubbing his hands together warming them.

They gave him a weird look but put the pack away, closing the hatch. "So?"

"Hang on. Where does it hurt?"

"I've been kicked in the stomach. Only one they got in." They sighed, closing their eyes. Tommy narrowed his eyes, putting his hands on their stomach, releasing the built-up energy. As he did, he could sense everything inside this person's torso. It was confusing. Not what he expected.

An audible sigh of relief came from them as they relaxed. He could see it was working.

"That should do it." He said after a moment, taking his hands off. "So uh. It's uh, I didn't catch your name. I mean, they called you Spira but..."

"Orchid Spira."

Oh shit. Tommy was in the same car as Orchid Spira. His blood suddenly ran cold.

"Orchid. Spira." He repeated. "I mean, that sounded familiar, but hah, who listens to rumours, right? The one who murdered their husband and then went to town bowling with his head. Hahaha. How imaginative are people."

"That wasn't invented. He cheated on me with the owner of the bowling lane. However that's not why I killed him. But you wouldn't care."

A moment's silence and Tommy realised that he didn't want to ask.

"So is it true you're from Lhoorl?"

"Born and raised." Raindrops started dancing on the pod glass, so Orchid turned on the engine and reversed away from the men, slowly getting themselves back together.

"But you're not-"

"No, I'm human. Everyone knows the story of the lost cosmonauts who settled on Lhoorl. Those were my ancestors. Mind you, there are not many 100% pure humans on that planet anymore, and we've inserted our genes into their pool. Probably why the Lhoorlians are so fucked up. I mean, they're already bad, then mix that with a bunch of Russians crazy enough to let themselves be shot into space with a hope, a prayer and an old fashioned combustion engine."

Tommy shivered. "So.... That's a very interesting story. Maybe I should go home."

"You wanted to ask me something when you came down. What was it?" Interrupted Orchid.

Tommy glanced outside into the falling rain.

"I want you to teach me how to fight like you do."

Chapter Fourteen
Orchid agrees to Teach

"First things first." Orchid looked over. "What is it you want to do?" They asked.

"To protect people." Said Tommy without thinking.

Orchid scoffed. "Oh, you're serious?" They cleared their throat and drove the pod towards their own mansion.

"Yes I'm serious!" Tommy said, looking over. "And... During my last pick up, someone... was on the ship. A Lhoorlian." The lights of the city started flickering over them as the pod made its way back to the centre. Here, the lights were somehow brighter and more modern, and Tommy felt a pang of jealousy comparing it to his own block of flats.

The pod slid into an underground garage.

"So do you know who attacked you?"

"No, and I don't really care." Orchid slipped out of the car. If the seats were just the right size for Tommy, Orchid's slighter form could fit in them twice. Still, they moved with a grace that showed they had definitely had some training. Tommy got out of the car.

If the stories of Lhoorl were right, this person had probably fought before going to earth... before ending up way out back here. To have lived on three different planets, that thought just stunned Tommy.

"So uh, you live here?" He glanced around.

Orchid scoffed again and called for an elevator. "Come on in."

Following Orchid took him to a large open space, about as large as the car park they had slid into. The whole space was devoid of walls, with thick glass that seemed to have screens – most of the screens were currently down. There was a large workbench, but also a lovely kitchen that Tommy just loved. Besides that you could find all the expected comforts of a bathroom, lounge and a large bed. This person lived alone on this floor, Tommy thought, wondering how one would get such a spot assigned to them. Orchid was definitely not the kind of person Tommy would have welcomed to the planet.

That thought again rocked his world. Perhaps Cattori Five was not as egalitarian as they were made to believe.

"Do you know how to fight?"

"No." Tommy replied.

"Are you good at running?"

"Somewhat." Admitted Tommy. Orchid glanced over his form and he blushed.

"Right. You have a lot to learn." Orchid sighed and opened the fridge.

Chapter Fifteen
Tommy goes to see his Mother

Tommy almost fell out of the pod. Getting to the remote farm his mother tended had taken the better part of three days. He'd started by taking the basic public transport options. By the morning of day three, he had given up and requested a temporary motorised vehicle license and a rental pod. The last few hours were spent driving the distance to the farm.

The farming fields had rolled into view steadily after the first day's drive. By day two, there was more field than city, and now on day three, it looked like this place was wild and unkempt. The way it must have looked before colonisation. But then a probe would fly overhead and disturb his isolated reveries.

The smell of lavender greeted him from the edges of the farm, and it made him smile. These were the smells of childhood. He grew up here until they moved to the city to get him an education. It was nice to be back out here, where he didn't have to worry about shady coworkers and intrigue.

He parked the pod and locked it before walking into the farm. It was huge. He could see why his mother loved it here. The silence was heavenly. The air was clean, and small animals darted in and out of the bushes all around the beautiful farm—mostly small rodents who kept the heavy tangle of the brush in check.

"Tommy!" Chrissy waved from the driveway. Her long-form was clad in handmade overalls - he could tell from the wonky hemming. But who here would even care, except for the patrol drones?

Rushing over to hug her. "Mum!" Laughing and hugging her close.

"Look at you!" She made a bit of a face at the nuskin on his face. "Tsk. At least it looks like it's healing."

"Don't worry. It is. In a few days, you won't see it." He kissed her cheek. "The lavender is gorgeous this year."

"Yes! It's a good harvest. It'll make us a pretty penny." She replied, walking inside, and he followed.

"I love it when you visit. Too bad you have to use your sick leave."

"Honestly. It's fine. If I can stay the night at least." He wasn't sure how strict they were about the curfews here.

"Your room is ready. Don't worry. Dinner is at five pm, and breakfast at six am." She explained the house schedule.

Calamity at Cattori V

"Great." He nodded. Getting up that early did not sound great, but he was sure he could manage for one day.

"So tell me how my son has been! That accident gave me such a fright." She shook her head. "Let me make some tea."

"It's just an accident. They happen." He shrugged. "It was just lucky nobody got hurt worse." Walking into the kitchen, he could smell the stew on the stove, and it was beautiful.

"I'm okay. I promise." He said, tearing his eyes away from the stove. So little had changed since his childhood.

"So it didn't have anything to do with..." She pointed up, and he sighed.

"No." She was probably the one person in the world who had somewhat of an idea of what had happened to him, and she didn't know half of it. All she knew was that he had returned with some kind of healing powers, but she had urged him to keep his head down.

"I... was escorting someone. They attacked us. The pod crashed and... Well." He sighed. It still was hard to go mentally back to that moment.

"And your face," she asked, shaking her head. "You'll never find a good other half like that!"

"Mum!" He tsked, making a face. "I'm not thinking about that stuff that much..." He had to admit. "I just... You know what happened and that I..."

Trying to put it into words without sounding insane. That I can now heal people? That I'm using that in real life to go out and fight?

"You can't get distracted." She put the kettle onto the induction stove. "All I want for you is to be happy and to get off of this planet. Please promise me that." She looked up. "Please promise me you won't jeopardise your future. On Earth, you'd be able to have fun with..." She moved her hands towards him.

"But here? We're all watched. All considered criminals, even the few of us that aren't."

He bit his lip. Despite his status giving him some advantages, he had to admit his mother was right. Curfew still counted for him, and he had to take care to play an active role in society as was demanded of him.

"I'm sending in my applications soon. I'm not losing track of anything." He promised, kissing her forehead. The last time he had been here, her forehead had come to his nose, and now he was almost leaning over to kiss it. He wondered if he had grown or if she was shrinking with age, and he hoped for the first.

"Good boy." chuckling, she placed some tea into the old ceramic pot by the stove. "You know, there are three kids born this year. I wonder if it's the farm life but..." She laughed a little. It was a joyous thing, but he still felt a bit bad for them.

"Will they grow up here?"

"Probably! I mean, when you were a kid, the other kids had been born in the city, so we had to move there once you had to start higher schooling. But it seems the majority of them are born here now, so we'll likely have the school starting here." She nodded. Pouring the hot water slowly into the pot.

"The farms seem to be doing well."

"We're thriving." Chris replied proudly. "Our tea exports are getting so big that surpluses may be sent to Earth if the CCC approves of the planning. I mean, it's the perfect product. It will definitely survive the long journey, with the right preparations, maybe even dry on the ship. I can volunteer to go along." Chrissy winked. "Oh! You haven't heard! I haven't told you!"

"No, what is it?" Clearly good news as she bustled to find a towel to wipe her hands.

"I've gotten a letter. Me and a few of the older people here are being released to Earth. Of course, similar setup to here. We'll be tending a farm somewhere in the American Continent, but we'll be back on Earth! So you must get your papers sorted, alright?"

He blinked. "You better not beat me to earth!" He joked, his heart sinking. His mother would no longer be here, so he would no longer have an excuse to stay.

"But how, is it something new they're trying?" He peeked over to the letter, seeing the familiar CCC and Corrections Department letterheads. It looked real.

"Yes, it seems they're thinking of rehabilitating some of us low-risk criminals. You forget your mum was just an old fashioned hustler." She smiled. "This is no hustle, though. Paperwork is legit, and I checked it. Can't scam a scammer." She put the towel down and poured the tea into two cups. "Let's drink to earth." She nodded.

Tommy nodded. "Wow. It'll be a whole new start for you." He picked up the cup she held out to him.

"And at my age." Shaking her head. "But I look forward to it! It'll be the same kind of farm I've been told, and we'll be growing wheat. To be honest, the tea trade is growing a little old. I miss good coffee, as well."

He chuckled. He'd had coffee once and had not been impressed by it, but one day he wanted to try the Earth's version of it.

"I'm really happy for you." He smiled.

"When you get to earth, come find me, okay?" Chrissy sitting down by him. "I know this is big, and it'll probably mean we won't see each other for a few years... But I love you so much." She put a hand on his. "I just... I can't waste this opportunity. It was made very clear to me that it was this or nothing." She licked her lips.

"You should go!" He smiled. "It's good. It's... wow. I'm really happy for you... But..."

"I know. It's hard to believe. There's never been a return flight for any convict. But... Perhaps they just don't want me here at retirement age. You forget, being here used to shorten our life spans quite a bit, but now we're all growing older." She nodded and squeezed his hand before sitting back. As he glanced over, he wondered what did happen to people of retirement age on the planet, the ones who could no longer keep themselves busy.

"I guess that's it." He chuckled. "I really will come find you, mum. But I may not get to Earth any time soon."

"Nonsense. When you apply, you'll probably be given fast track priority!" She waved her hand.

"I hope so." That all depended on whether or not he got a second Warning.

"You know, if you came clean about what happened... They might remove the Warning from your record."

"I doubt it." Chuckling, he looked over. "I never even told you the whole story, mum. It's hard. I don't think anyone would ever believe it."

She blinked. "Tell me."

So he did.

To her credit, she listened, keeping her gaze level all the way through until he was done.

"That's... something," She said at the end. "A race of tiny aliens that has never come forward." She couldn't help chuckling. "But I think they did this for a reason, and I don't think that reason is here."

"But this is home, mum." He heard himself say, blinking away the confusion. "Oh. I mean, I..."

"I know what you mean." Smiling, she reached out, touching his cheek, a serene smile on her face, even though what he had told her must have disturbed her. He remembered growing up, peeking into the parlour when she won large stacks of credits in illicit poker games. Her face had never wavered or flinched, but somehow, it was more open to him.

"This is the only world you know, and trust me when I say, Earth will be very different and not always for the better. But we'll be free." Nodding as the sound of the patrol drone approached. Out here, without the city noise, it was easy to hear the oppressive droning of its engines. His mum sighed as it faded away again.

"Promise me you won't endanger your chances of getting to Earth. Please."

He licked his lips but then nodded. "Promise."

Chapter Sixteen

Back to Work

Tommy walked in to work a few weeks later, the nu skin fully healed, and the cast removed. His face barely showed a trace of the large wound it had been just a few weeks prior. He'd been advised careful exercise, though he wasn't sure if that was because of his recent injuries or weight.

He waved his arms. "Hey! Look pa, no cast."

"So proud of you, son." Laughed Lion, still sitting back. "Almost missed you. It was boring here by myself."

"I'm sure you found something to occupy yourself." Tommy sat down, dressed in a nice shirt and pants.

"I cleaned your desk, boss' orders." Lion took his feet off of his own desk. "It was a mess."

"Aw! I was saving that free lunch coupon." Frowned Tommy, looking around where everything was. Not that there was much in there, some personal items, one photo of him with his mother he kept forgetting to take home. It was still where he left it, but most of the junk had been cleared.

"Don't worry, I used that on an earth style corn dog." He stood up and rolled his head in his neck.

"Was it good, at least?" Tommy started up his work terminal.

"The absolute best."

Tommy groaned. "You owe me one of those now."

"We'll get some for lunch. How are you feeling?" Lion replied.

"Ready to get back to it, honestly." Tommy blinked. "I've been bored stiff."

"I bet you have." Lion looked away.

Over the last few weeks, Tommy had spent more covert time with Orchid Spira. There was a lot to learn – not just about fighting but about Lhoorlian culture. When Orchid had heard the story about the pod crash, on had insisted he learn about Lhoorlians. Lhoorlian fighting, Lhoorlian society, even their pronouns – she, he and on. On was the one Orchid used, though Tommy wondered how many people knew on personally enough to know that.

He'd been working out with the other, learning how to fight. Some fat had turned into muscle. Tommy was not going to be too joyous about that just yet. And though their banter was still the same, he noticed Lion glancing over more than before. Had he discerned the change? Or was it something else?

Calamity at Cattori V

"Nothing's changed here then?" Tommy glanced up at the broken surveillance camera, though he kind of liked it that way.

"Not a thing." replied Lion stretching out, before getting up.

He walked over to the coffee and tea station near their desk. As usual, they were almost out of tea, but there was plenty of coffee.

"Want a cup?"

"Yes, please, tea, splash of soy milk."

"No sugar anymore?" Lion frowned.

"Nah, I had a doughnut for breakfast. Two."

"Alright, I don't think the one lump of sugar will make a difference at that point, but it's your cuppa." He laughed and brought over the two mugs.

"Thanks." Said Tommy, sipping the tea.

Lion, apparently feeling adventurous, had grabbed some coffee. "Can report the coffee is still horrid." Regret twisted Lion's face with his first sip and he got up to pour it out.

"Glad it's still terrible. I was worried I'd missed something." Tommy chuckling at his partner's folly.

"Nah." Shrugged Lion. "Are you being reassigned to casework?" Lion asked, glancing over as he poured himself a cup of tea. Putting on a kettle for the next person. Strange how even in a penal colony, those small office rules applied. Clean up after yourself. Fill the kettle. Fight the sense of impending doom.

"Yes, but it's mostly paperwork for the moment. They don't want me out in the field until the psych signs off on me." Shaking his head. "I should have taken more time off."

"Don't be silly. You'd just be moping at home." Lion replied. "Did you see that hot girl again?"

Tommy blinked. "Violet? No, I mean. I don't think she was into me like that..." Clearing his throat, he sighed. "I don't... think people get into me like that."

Lion shrugged. "You'd be surprised. Anyway. I'm in the same boat. With the psych, I mean. I do think people find me attractive-"

"What about the fugitive, Tattek?" Asked Tommy. This was not a line of conversation he was pleased about.

"Assigned a new caseworker. He's doing okay, last I heard, and he'll be coming in some time this week to get his paperwork." Answered Lion.

It seemed like he wasn't the only one who'd wondered about their ex-charge. Something was wrong. Why had a Lhoorlian been brought to the planet, coming under increasing control of the opaque CCC? Was it another power grab, or were they somehow hoping to make money off of this?

Tommy put his mug down and got up. "Time to actually do some of that dreaded paperwork. I'll see you later."

"Later." Lion agreed. "I've gotta scrounge some breakfast together out of whatever we've got around."

Tommy winced at that. "You left the house without eating?"

Lion raised an eyebrow and looking like he was about to say something. Still, perhaps he was saved by the AI monitoring their interactions.

"Yeah. It's how I keep my beautiful figure. Now scram while I turn some sugar packets into something edible."

Snorting, Tommy walked back to his desk, shaking his head. Lion's desk was on the edge of his periphery view while sitting at his desk, and it was the furthest from the entrance. But he could see the man quickly typing something before tapping send. Tommy suppressed some shivers. He had read it and now was working hard not to show his nerves. Furiously whipping his head back to his own terminal.

It had read, "Orchid has onis talons in Tommy. Caution advised. Will continue to monitor."

Chapter Seventeen
Training with Orchid

The first day back at work had been about as exciting as Tommy had expected: not at all.

Paperwork mainly consisting of older cases, people who had been long since integrated needing follow up. So most of the day was spent contacting them, writing updates in their files, going onto the next one. Rinse and repeat. It was nice and mindless, at least, and Tommy was happy that some of the ones he'd followed up on were people he had helped integrate earlier.

The day ended. Gathering up updated case files in his arms, he brought them down to the archives, showing his badge before he was allowed into the underground storage with the tablets.

He sauntered through the walkways, putting the data tablets back in their designated place. They clicked back in place with a satisfying sound, and a slight whir as Cerebellum accessed them to update the central memory.

After slotting the last one into place, Tommy hesitated.

He'd found out what happened to Jack Tattek but never about what had happened with the Lhoorlian. He didn't even remember the name and couldn't find the case number. It seemed so stupid. Had he known what kind of significance that encounter would play, he would have memorised every detail.

Walking to a hub display and tapping in the welcoming date and his ID, searching to see if the file he had seen that day was still in the archive or if it was active somewhere.

Surely that couldn't do any harm? The therapist had encouraged him to ask questions, and if he was not allowed, he would just... leave it. No harm, no foul.

A result popped up, though the name of the Lhoorlian had been redacted, with only the two human prisoners mentioned as Jack Tattek and Cecil Berukko. The accident's cause was now listed as a simple collision after the pod's navigation had gone haywire. Doubt entered his mind for a moment, strange he doubted himself, but Lion had been there, and he'd seen the Lhoorlian as well.

Closing the file and logging out of his session, he walked to the exit. He wasn't exactly the world's greatest spy, but he had very little to hide here. The computer chimed, noting his brief access. It then powered down the display as he walked away from the terminal.

No alarms blaring, no lights flashing. Perhaps Tommy had gotten away with tiptoeing the line on this occasion.

Luckily, this area was beyond his supervisor Belinda's terrain - her AI security clearance was simply not high enough. While AIs were not meant to realise such facts, she did mention them quite often. Part of her personality, he guessed.

Or maybe she just didn't like being down here. Cerebellum did not have a voice like Belinda, but she was very intimidating. The computer could gather a person's data in its entirety, all from a single digital footprint. It could just look you up and down, knowing everything there was to know about you, projecting out models. He had stashed ideas of looking up Tattek or the incident report, as he didn't want to set her off.

But this was mighty strange already. Why was the Lhoorlian no longer mentioned in the file? Licking his lips, he punched the button to call for an elevator up. Alone here, so near to the supercomputer, even he was starting to feel nervous. The elevator doors slid open, and he stepped inside, glad to get away from the cooled archive room.

Tommy saw a led briefly blinking as the elevator door closed, Cerebellum noting his departure time. He had been spotted and cautioned, or at least it felt like that. A shiver ran through him. It's just a computer, not an evil mastermind. Get a freaking grip.

He wasn't sure why the computer scared him the way it did when he was literally training with a pink-haired psychopath. Every evening since their first meeting, he had snuck out to mansion to train with on. Of course, with his arm in the sling, it had been a lot of theory at first. Once outside the building, the feeling of dread lessened, and he was really happy for it. Walking to a subway, he boarded the first train towards Orchid's flat.

The large apartment building stood at the edge of the suburb closest to town. It was part of some of the more expensive developments in the area. It was as close to a gated community as one could get on a prison planet. They were all meant to be equal, but of course, the more valuable you were to the CCC, the more you could swing. And clearly, Orchid had something to offer... Tommy wondered what that was.

Looking up, the apartment building appeared into view. Brutalist fashion, old earth style, all hard concrete and edges probably because it was cheap and imposing. Despite the plain frontage, the whole block had been made with luxury in mind. Still stark enough to remind them this was meant to be where they redeemed themselves. Or something. The station was almost empty – most people living in this area had pods and licenses for them. Wondering briefly if Orchid had managed to get onis pod repaired without too many questions? But who was going to ask one of the most notorious people on the planet questions?

Reaching to press the buzzer, the door opened before he could press the button to be buzzed in. The doorman stared at his finger.

"Spira is expecting you. The buzzer is broken, I'm afraid. It won't stop if you push it." He made a face. "And we'd rather not hear it all night."

"I'm guessing this block doesn't get many visitors then."

"No. But uh, personally, I'm happy to see Orchid is getting a little on the side, if you know what I mean. Keeps On happy."

He took a moment, his eyes going wide. "Oh. OH." Tommy swallowed. "Yes. That's uh... On is... good." Nodding, better for people to think they were lovers than anything else. That way, nobody questioned why they spent the night, and hey, it was not illegal after all.

He called the elevator quickly to try and get away from the doorman's smile. This was mildly uncomfortable. Who even had a concierge? It made him wonder if the doorman worked for the CCC or one of the residents and hoped he worked for the latter.

"You're early." Orchid looked up as he entered. On stood naked, having just left the shower, using the hot air blowers in the wall to dry off. Orchid's body was as well known to him as his own by now.

"You know the drill." Orchid looked over.

Sighing, he took his clothes off, as well. He was still convinced Orchid was paranoid, thinking they were being watched and listened to unless they were naked or having sex. Programmed privacy.

Calamity at Cattori V

"Now that you're healed, we can actually start on some actual training."

"So what did you call all that damn weightlifting and running on treadmills?" Tommy groaned, not looking forward to more aching muscles.

"Shush. Start with your run." Orchid nodding to the treadmill. Tommy launched it, starting with a slow run. If Orchid did the same routine, it would really pay off. Onis frame was thin and wiry but with a strength that was hard to believe.

"When can I start... doing things?" Tommy panted between breaths as he ran.

"When you get fast enough to outrun the drones. Seven kilometres an hour? Move that up to eleven." On looked over the display of the treadmill and adjusted the speed.

Tommy groaned. "I wanted to be able to talk!" He defended, though he knew he couldn't cheat.

"So... when?"

"A few more weeks. We'll need to teach you how to fight properly." On looked over. "Also, your company offered me a job as a Lhoorlian translator and cultural expert."

Tommy almost fell off the treadmill. "They may just want you to talk to the Lhoorlian!"

"Which one?" On asked, raising an eyebrow. "There are many of those."

"There is one on this planet." He hissed and climbed up the treadmill incline again. "The accident. I looked it up. They captured him, and he's no longer mentioned in the incident report."

"Probably thrown out of a spaceship. Really, it's what he would have wanted." Orchid quipped, voice dripping with sarcasm.

"I'm getting there's not much love lost there." Tommy noticed, working hard to keep up with the treadmill.

Orchid slammed the stop button on the machine. Tommy stumbled.

"Do you know how long the latest war has been going? Since before I was born. I was running from troops as soon as I learned to walk. I fought as early as fifteen. And you know how tough those bastards are. I lived it until I was twenty-nine and managed to get to Earth as a refugee."

"Where you immediately decided to kill -"

"It's all I know, Tommy!" Orchid said, taking a deep breath. "You want to learn to fight? You ask me. You won't learn how to live a good life from me, though."

"Understood." Nodding, taking a deep breath. "Thanks. I do appreciate your help in this."

Orchid rolled onis eyes. "You can drop the emotional baggage at the door next time."

"Tell me about the war?" asked Tommy.

Calamity at Cattori V

"No." Orchid looked at the treadmill and started it up again. "Finish your run."

Groaning and turning the dial back up to eleven. It was hard to forget this person was unstable, and he had to be careful pushing on. "I need to leave early today. I need to go find someone." Taking deep breaths, trying to hide how short of breath he was getting.

"Alright, I think you're able to do something stupid like that. Who?"

"Someone who was in the car when the accident happened." Gasping and lowering the speed. "Can't keep up, can't keep up!"

"Fine. Slow down, but don't stop." Orchid ordered. "Also. I have something to give you," Orchid continued. "Took a while to get it made..."

A while? Watching Orchid fetch a large box. Three weeks wasn't exactly a very long time. Especially not for something that size. He watched Orchid tap it open. It held a full-body black suit with strategic plates of bulletproof plastic. The top half had a helmet with a mask built-in, which didn't even look too naff. There were metal leg braces, which he guessed assisted in running.

"Oh, we're making this vigilante thing official now?" A chuckle.

"You'll need body armour, and you try finding any outside of the CCC and no offence..." Orchid looked him over. "But in your size as well. Try it on, then put it back. Don't get any ideas about this yet."

Two hours later, Tommy left the apartment in Orchid's pod. Because it was opaque, it was hard to tell who was inside, and he just hoped he wouldn't be stopped. Tattek didn't live far away, and Tommy just needed to talk to him for a moment. This had not been thought through very much, but he needed to do this. Time was running short – the longer he waited, the more the details of all of this would be buried.

Tattek's flat was a stark contrast to Orchid's. An old TV lay broken on the kerb in front of the building. Further into the suburbs, if not for the curfew, it would have only been a short walk. This place clearly had less money pumped into it – the buildings were older and smaller, and the streets were littered with trash. Gingerly parking the pod and getting out.

The smell was different, too—more of a pronounced cooking smell. Fumbling for the correct doorbell, Tommy was quickly buzzed in. Rushing inside, closing the outer door and pausing, listening for drones. At the top of the stairs, a few people were peeking out of their doors.

"I'm looking for Jack Tattek." He said, getting up. "As a friend." In his nice clothes, he probably stood out like a sore thumb.

"Um. Hi - oooh. I remember you!" Tattek opened his door wider. "I uh, sorry. We sometimes buzz people in just because they get caught out in the dark. I didn't think you were actually there to see someone, you know." Jack chuckling a little nervously. He looked decent - he had new joggers on with a sweater. The smell of cooking seemed to be coming from his apartment, as well.

"Hi. I'm Tommy Terrengan. I was meant to help you settle in. I'm glad to see you're doing okay."

"Yeah. They uh, assigned me someone else, and they did all the things. Come in." Jack leading him inside the apartment.

"What's cooking?" Tommy asked.

"Oh! I made moussaka." A note of pride in his voice. "I found some lamb at one of the stores and... couldn't resist. Childish comfort food, you know?"

Nodding, Tommy added, "mine's mac and cheese. It used to be really hard to get cheese, so... It was a real treat," sighing in memory.

"Yeah." Nodded Jack. "I'd offer you some, but it needs some oven time still."

"No, it's fine," shaking his head. "I uh. I wanted to ask you about the accident."

"Mmm. I've talked about that a lot. Nobody seems to take it very seriously."

"Yeah. I was meaning to ask about the Lhoorlian."

"That bit was peculiar, you know?" Jack looking over, lifting his kettle up. "Tea?"

"Sure. Chamomile if you have it? So what about the alien?" Trying not to sound as impatient as he felt.

Jack nodded as he poured some hot water into the mugs. "He was kept separate from us. Nobody saw him all trip and then suddenly at the end of the trip... It seemed chaotic. The guard thought he was with us. Someone else thought he was meant to go elsewhere. Usually, this company is much more efficient." Jack paused, shaking his head. Something appeared to bother him.

"Ah! Anyway, I never thought about it beyond that much, and then there was that crash. I told them the alien wasn't meant to be with us. I think they made a mistake, you know." Bringing over a mug with a teabag of chamomile in it and handing it to Tommy.

"Thank you. I think you're right, for what it's worth," said Tommy.

The whirr of a drone sounded outside, and Tommy shivered. It was quiet until the drone noise subsided.

"Alright. I think you should go." Tattek said softly. "But thank you so much. It's nice that you cared and you were... really nice when I met you. Still are. Heh."

Sighing, he had more questions, so many more, but the man was right. He was tiptoeing the line here. Somewhere, this all pointed to something, and he wasn't sure what yet.

"Yes, goodnight." He took a quick sip of the tea and then headed for the door.

"Stay safe, Mr Tattek."

Tattek chuckled, opening the door for him. "Haven't been mistered in a while."

"Alright, good night."

"Good night." Tattek wished him, mug in hand. This time the neighbours' doors remained closed, which was probably for the best. Nothing notable happened, so they probably would never mention this and forget it eventually.

Who knew being a vigilante sometimes required this much banality?

Chapter Eighteen
The First Incident

Tommy yawning as he woke up. Short nights were becoming a real issue for him. Staggering to the kitchen and starting the kettle, he tried to figure out what he wanted for breakfast. Something simple, probably. Filling a small bowl with dried fruits and spooning a blob of yoghurt on top of it.

Orchid had been lecturing him on eating better, and he had to admit it helped. Though he'd already been eating pretty healthily, he just added more nuts, fruit and vegetables to his diet. It also covered the extra calories he needed for the training without arousing too much suspicion.

Yawning and stirring some oats into the contraption he was calling breakfast, not even sure this would work in any sane way. Moving around nuts and yoghurt with his spoon until it became a passable bircher, he sat down with the bowl, looking around his small apartment. The space was small, only a few rooms, but it met his needs. Some

Calamity at Cattori V

days it felt claustrophobic, though. Sighing and looking at the clock between bites.

Thinking back to the night before, he had stayed with Orchid until two am, training and trying to puzzle this whole thing together. Orchid had felt there was probably nothing to it. Weird things happen every day that didn't arouse suspicion, so why did this?

Shaking his head, something was wrong. He'd grown up on this planet, and he could just tell. Who knew how many Lhoorlians had been brought here, then vanished without a trace. Why? Were they training them for law enforcement? A brainwashed killing machine to sell to Earth. Some weaponised prison planet? Or was he just wrong, and was all this just... coincidence?

A statistical anomaly, one alien on a planet of thousands, shipped back before anyone could tell anything was wrong? Centauri Care Concern wasn't the infallible being it pretended to be.

The fragrance of tea filled the apartment. For a second, convincing him, maybe life hadn't changed since the abduction, but... he still knew it had.

Pouring his tea, a gentle flow into the cup, when suddenly a shockwave went through the building. The cup bouncing to the floor. Moving his foot fast as a spray of hot tea landed where his foot was. A loud rumbling came through his feet, and he ducked just as the windows broke, feeling the vibrations through the prefab wooden floors. His mug rolling away as the puddle of tea vibrated along with the floor. Droplets shooting up.

Damn. What happened?

Fuck! Covering his ears as sound returned with an overwhelming noise of alarms going off. The planetary PA system took over to spread a message. Over the entire planet's personal devices, public speakers at important crossroads, and anything else that could squawk out the news.

"Please remain calm. A meteorite has struck the planet. There has been damage to major infrastructure, and we are working hard to restore power. Looting will be strongly punished. Please remain calm. A meteorite has..." The loop continued.

Only now realising the power was off. It was dark, and only the screens outside and the emergency broadcast enabled devices were working. Taking a deep breath and shakily standing up.

"The hell just happened?" He nervously asked himself, looking out his window. The communication hub in his living room switched on. Power seemed to be returning in a small capacity.

"CCC Employee. If your flat is structurally sound, please remain inside until you hear further instructions. Food will be delivered to every building, and power will be back on as soon as possible. Please remain calm."

Calamity at Cattori V

"Calm." Laughing and looking around, first and foremost, he would need to cover the windows. This was a planet of outlaws, and looting would occur no matter how strongly it was discouraged. If the power was off, there were no cameras. The drones already had a limited range on battery power if they were unable to recharge, so they would be deployed very sparingly.

He had some wood board somewhere. With shaking hands, gathering the shattered glass from the fallen cup and clearing it up so he could board up the windows. It felt weird. Where had they been struck? It had to have been close. He had nails somewhere. With shaking hands, trying to find both items before cursing and sagging down to the floor. What was he doing? Boards wouldn't keep out burglars... much.

Maybe staying inside wasn't a good idea. People were bound to be hurt and... Oh gosh. He was considering it, wasn't he? The box with the suit was lying on his kitchen table, where he had left it the night before. If Orchid's power was still on, which was very likely, the suit's tracker stations and comms would be working. Orchid had generators in onis basement. He had seen them.

Shaking his head, he started putting on the outfit, starting with the pants with inbuilt grip boots, before putting on the jacket and the helmet. It powered on with a soft whirr.

"Orchid. Orchid, are you there?"

"Not the best time. What is it?"

"Have you got power?"

"Obviously, but the generator won't last long, and there's already looters knocking." The clang of metal rang over the call. "I need to arm up."

"Don't kill -"

"If anyone comes for me, I will," Orchid said. "You - Hold." The feed was cut for a second. "I need to go now. CCC orders me to evacuate to their headquarters. You do what you need to do, but I can't back you up. Be careful."

That was weird. Why were the rich folk being asked to evacuate? They were the ones safest during an attack, what with the gated community and their personal guards. Tasers didn't go out when the power went out.

Again that nagging feeling there was something more. Something he wasn't getting.

The hub chimed again. Lion was trying to reach him via his home AI. He quickly shoved the helmet and suit out of sight, wrapping himself up in a blanket and only then answered.

"Tommy! Tell me you're still safe at home and not stuck somewhere." Lion's face was pale, even accounting for the lousy camera on these devices.

"I'm at home. Where are you?" Looking out his window at the chaos that was happening.

"I was at work early. CCC is having everyone stay where they are until they can get everything sorted." Lion said.

Calamity at Cattori V

"At least in your area." He added quickly.

"Where did it hit?" Tommy asked. "I'm not seeing it outside, but it must have been close!"

"No idea. It's chaos right now." Lion sighed and looked over. "Look, stay put. We're sending out security and safety people."

"Yeah. I'm not going anywhere." Tommy lied as he glanced out the window. A few wounded people were already staggering outside, and a few buildings looked close to collapsing. There was no way they would get here fast enough to help anyone out.

"Look, I gotta go. I mean, I gotta stay put. But I've got something on the stove."

"What? The power is out everywh-"

Tommy turned off the feed and sighed, sitting down on the floor to finish putting on his get-up. These were not ideal circumstances, especially not with Orchid not there to help. Still, he had to do something. He had the power to help out. Shuffling the top on and adjusting the bracers, a tedious job he had to do strap by strap. It gave him time to think. The fact that Lion had been at work early was... strange, to say the least. It was still very early in the morning. And the man was hiding more than a suddenly earnest work ethic. Did -

Orchid said "I evacuate". Not we. So Orchid was on onis way to the office building where Lion was. Was that a coincidence? He shivered. Once the straps and plates were all on, he had to admit it made him feel powerful. There was nothing squishy about him in this get-up. The plates were designed for extra support and flattening bulges, and he almost looked trim and athletic. Rather than flabby with perhaps some musculature underneath. Taking a deep breath and walking over to the door before pausing. How was he going to get out without people noticing? And how would he make his way back? The roof. From there, he could take the fire escape down.

He shoved some shorts and a sweater in a backpack and then leaned out his door. The hall was clear. This whole endeavour was so spur of the moment that he felt like an idiot. It was in motion now, and he was getting it done. He had to go for it now, or he felt like he never would, after a quick check of the area. Rushing to the stairs, running up them towards the roof.

Pushing the roof access door open, sound washed over him, a clear view of the city stretched all around. Small fires had started, and an older building had collapsed, probably unable to withstand the shockwave? Or worse, having been where the meteorite had struck? People clambering around the wreckage and drones converging to get footage for the arriving rescue people. But it didn't look like a meteorite.

Making his way down the fire escape towards the hit building, mind racing. A spaceship? Once, ten years ago, their farm had been struck by space debris. Back then, clearly visible in the crater was the giant rock that had

Calamity at Cattori V

struck them. This was just destruction.

High up in the atmosphere, a spaceship hanging was over them, almost invisible to the naked eye. He could just about hear it as it powered up the engines to take off. The sound chilling him to his core.

It didn't look like the usual earth hauliers that brought prisoners? Even then, none were scheduled for another month. Maybe a resupply ship? Those always came very secretively to make sure they weren't targeted by any mobs trying to steal goods.

Running down the stairs and pushing on towards the stricken building. The get-up was made for nighttime wear, not daytime. He stood out like a sore thumb.

"Hey! Are you here to help us?" Someone called out. "He's broken something."

Steering towards the voice and crouching down by an injured man lying in a woman's lap, barely stirring to breathe. Looked like some badly broken ribs. Placing hands on the man's chest, he let the healing energy go through them, concentrating. Quickly he could hear the man breathe easier. It was much less ragged, the man's eyes closing in relief instead of bulging.

"Keep him lying down until help gets here." Blinking in surprise, Tommy's voice sounding deeper than he was used to. Then walking away towards the next person who needed help. The wounded were lined up by the base of what used to be a building, but he could not see any space debris that would indicate what had happened here even up close.

This wasn't a meteorite, he thought, looking around. However, right now, he needed his mental capacity to focus on healing. Rushing around and stabilising some people, healing others fully. Finally, after about twenty minutes, official rescuers started arriving. Efficiently as always, small teams spread around the debris and started triaging, sticking coloured dots on people's clothes depending on the severity of the cases. Tommy proudly considered that perhaps thanks to him, there were fewer red dots than one would expect. Or maybe they all died, a mean voice inside him said. Shivering, he started walking off.

"Hey, you!" A voice called out. "All in black. Do you have any ID on you?"

He kept walking, hoping it didn't come to a confrontation. Again. It would be the second time in a short period that he needed to run from questions, which really did not make him feel any better about it.

Picking up the pace, he heard footsteps behind him quickening and scanned for any hideouts he could nip into. There was a sewage pipe not too far up ahead, but it would be too small for him. Think, think. He needed some better options here.

The chance Violet would come out of nowhere again was pretty slim, but hey, maybe? Running around the block

Calamity at Cattori V

and disappearing into a service exit, pressing up against the corridor wall as he heard the footsteps go by.

"Check inside the building." A voice came through. Oh crap.

Throwing open the door, he started running again. Thinking about how surprisingly light this get-up was as the support tech kicked in, lifting strain from his knees, making running easier. It hadn't gotten a full charge, though, so he wasn't sure how long he could count on that. He would have to keep running for now but find somewhere else to hide.

Rounding the corner, trying to figure out a good way of keeping the most possible distance before they caught on. His ruse had already put some distance between them, but it wasn't going to last. They had the manpower to do a pincer manoeuvre, and he was, alas, on his own.

The town square was ahead, and then a roundel of eight streets he could maybe duck down. If he made it there? He would be in the open for a while, but then he could duck away and hopefully lose the trail.

They probably had reinforcements coming, though.

Closing his eyes, he kept running, tailgating into a building and rushing up the stairs despite someone's protests. He was not going to be caught. This was not how it was going to end.

Chapter Nineteen
The Resistance introduces Itself

Tommy had no idea how long he'd been running when the leg braces finally ran out. It wasn't that running suddenly became harder, but it did become slower and his spurts shorter. Taking a deep breath and resting against a container, amused that he seemed to have ended up at the port again. At least he had lost them. There were no more following drones or agents since he had left the town behind. Probably had been instructed to stay in particular quadrants and not to chase too far. He was not an important target in all this chaos.

What was he going to do? Getting back into town should be straightforward, but his get-up would be tagged. He had also not been smart enough to put anything on underneath, so while he had clothes with him in the backpack, he wasn't sure where he'd be able to stay out of sight long enough to get changed.

Suddenly he could hear the sound of an approaching pod. Holding his breath, he waited. Stopping in front of him, it was a bright red opaque pod built to seat five. Trying to decide, run or attack, when it folded open and revealed Violet.

"Keep running into you here." Violet winked. "Get in. You can get changed in the back if you want."

"You have a pod?" Wasting no time, getting in and waiting for the pod to close before taking the mask off. Sighing, he sat back. "So much better."

"You're welcome. It's not... mine per se," Violet added, chuckling. "I'll get it back before the owner knows it's missing."

Clambering to the back, shaking his head and asking, "Who are you?"

"Told you." Briefly turning her head to the backseat. "Violet."

"Watch where you're going." Shaking his head and taking his top off. It did not look like she was paying much attention to the road.

"Yeah but... There's a great show in the back."

"Eyes on the road. Not like you haven't seen it before. Also, you've seen it before." Sighing, he probably should feel more nervous that this dubious ally knew who he was. "And why are you... saving my butt?" He wondered aloud.

Silent for a moment, Violet answered, "I work for some people who have the best interest of the planet at heart."

Vague, but it sounded true enough.

Continuing, she added, "And those people believe you have the best interest of the planet at heart, as well."

"So you're... what? Anti CCC?" Frowning and slipping into the sweater he had packed.

"We just feel like... conditions have not improved for us as they should, considering how much money they are making off us. We're not just some kind of crop you grow to meet your needs. We're still people." She seemed earnest, and she was right. He'd been taught in school how on earth prisons had become privatised in some countries, which allowed the people who ran these facilities to make money off the prisoners' labour.

"Who committed horrific crimes. And why were you sent here?"

Violet dodged the question nimbly, "That's the thing, though. Fifty years ago, maybe one person every two or three years was brought here. Maybe two. Nowadays? We're seeing drops almost twice a year of groups as big as four or five."

"Because they want to optimise ships-"

"That's what they say. But that's still a big increase of people coming here. Now. Does that mean earth has become rife with psychopaths or that people are being sent here quicker? And if option two, would that have to do with CCC's growth and need for manpower?"

Shivering, his first thought had been not to even consider it. There was something to it. The CCC was good - to him.

But the natural-born population wasn't big enough to keep the factories and shops open.

"So... You think..."

"We do think something is going on. They're lobbying on earth to send criminals here for lesser convictions."

"That can't be something earth is okay with!" Calling out as he was wiggling into his shorts.

"Why not? You get to act like the people on your planet are all good. You just send away anyone who disagrees. But it's all one way, and that's what we're worried about. We can't just let people be sent here... Not for no good reason."

Nodding and mulling over what she had said. Maybe what she said made sense. It didn't track with Tommy's mum being sent back. Then again? Bringing older and less useful people, like his mum and her friends, back to earth. Or perhaps they just wanted to decrease the elderly population. But he didn't want to risk his mum's release by telling Violet she was being sent back to earth. Either way, not his problem.

"Well, whatever it is you think you're doing, I wish you luck. You can drop me off anywhere."

"You're just going to walk away?" Whipping her head back again, only looking back just in time to avoid crashing into a store.

"Why not? This is not my fight." Tommy answered.

"But you have a gift!" She cried out, looking back.

"Yes, and it helps individuals. I can't just link up with a group I have no idea about based on... a hunch!"

And that was generous. Even if his whole world view had just been shaken, he needed more proof. The fact that more people were being brought here wasn't enough. That could have only been a natural progression – none of them had any clue what earth was like these days, so any speculation of that nature was moot.

"Fine! I'll drop you off at your house, but I hope you join us some time."

Shaking his head, Tommy wanted to be clear. "I doubt it, Vi. Thank you for this, but I never asked for it."

"I still helped you because I think you're a good person. Nothing changes there." She slowed down near his apartment building.

Sighing, Tommy tried to finish gathering his gear. It was near impossible to shove all of the armour into his backpack. Settling for stowing the helmet in the bag and rolling up the clothes as best he could to look like a pile of laundry. It would need a wash regardless.

"Thanks for this anyway." Shuffling to the side, ready to get out, Violet smiled back at him.

"You're welcome. And wow. Have you been working out? It shows. Call Lion! He worries about you!"

"Goodnight, Violet." Climbing out of the pod with his gear. As soon as the door shut closed, she sped off. It was getting close to dark now and he would need to get inside. Watching her speed away, a stray thought wandered through his head again... What was the relationship between Lion and Violet? Was there any actual relationship?

Entering his apartment, dropping his bag, the helmet tumbled out. With shaking and tired hands, he slotted the helmet into the charger. After managing to click it in, he collapsed onto the sofa. In the end, it had been a good day, he'd helped people, and people were probably dying a little slower because he had stepped up. That was a nice thought.

Taking a deep breath and looking around the apartment, it was small, but it was his. He had worked to create it for himself. One day he would perhaps need to leave it all behind to go to earth, and the ships didn't exactly have much storage. He would happily leave stuff behind in the knowledge that someone else would live here and hopefully make something of his life's remnants. He licked his lips. Had what she said been true? Violet had said the deportations to Cattori Five had ramped up. If so, was that just a natural consequence of having an easy way to banish your enemies?

No. Tommy saw the records.

Most of them were murderers, robbers. She had to be wrong. But more people were coming here, and the planet was small. Food production was carefully balanced and a sudden influx.... Perhaps why his mother and others were brought back to earth?

Or maybe they were decommissioning Cattori Five?

No, that would never happen. Not if people were still being sent here. In that case, they would just stop sending people and instead just let everyone live out their lifespans here. He'd heard they didn't live as long here as on earth, as medical technology just wasn't that great.

He sat up. The sky was starting to darken. Sirens and cries had died down as the wounded were tended to, and the silent dead were gathered for disposal. No funerals on this planet. There were other ways to honour the dead, after all.

Grabbing his phone and trying Lion's desk phone number, hoping he was still at work or at least safe. Lion picked up after a few rings.

"Henry Lion." He said, clearly tired.

"Hey, it's me. Tommy." How redundant - he could tell Lion had recognised him from his relieved sigh. "Just wanted to check you were doing okay. You're still at work?"

"Yeah. We've been helping to coordinate the cleanup. Are you still at home?"

"Yeah. It's been crazy out there."

"It has been."

A silence followed. There was so much Tommy wanted to say about what he had done and what he could do, but he couldn't. Not over the phone. Before he could continue, Lion closed the conversation.

"Take care, Tommy. I need to get back to work."

"Yeah. Hopefully, we'll be back to normal business tomorrow."

"Hopefully," and with that, Lion hung up.

Tommy sighed. Stupid, stupid. What did he think he was going to achieve with that? This man was up to no good, and he could not trust him. Slowly but surely, the street lights outside twinkled on as things slowed down for the night. People would have locked up their houses tight - there was a good chance of looters trying to get at valuables while the security was spread out thin. Small gangs tended to form during crises like this, and it was best to stay out of their way.

Glancing at the helmet in the charger, the charging light blinking, he sighed. Unless you were a vigilante, he guessed.

Chapter Twenty
Tommy Helps Out

Last time there had been something anywhere nearly as bad as this, Tommy and his mother had holed up in the communal lounge of the farmhouse they were sharing. It had been a tense night, with the adults not sleeping and trying to muffle cries of surprise every time there was a bang or a crash outside, so they didn't wake him. He still remembered those whispers and the stifled sounds.

Perhaps his mother had known that the presence of her kid would help keep people calm. One group had kicked in the door, but seeing the huddled adults and a young kid, they had moved past and into the next place. Tommy had pretended to be asleep throughout it, but he'd hardly slept that night.

Tonight he was no longer the scared kid. He was well-armed and protected in his suit, though Orchid was still not responding on comms.

Clambering up to the roof again and looking around. At night, the streets were lit on regular nights, and it was generally quiet. But tonight, the power was still out, and

Calamity at Cattori V

the silence was almost absolute. Perhaps he had been wrong about the looters? Maybe it was still too early? The last of the rescuers and responders were pulling back, and after they were gone, it was anyone's guess what would happen. The final few pods filled with responders drove off, and then people started moving.

Tommy felt his eyes grow used to the dark as he stood on the roof, looking out at the people below. He'd only managed a partial charge of the helmet battery, so hopefully, there wasn't too much running and kicking. Sighing, starting the walk down the fire exit stairs and looking around. Nobody immediately running out to attack him, which he thought was a great start already.

Ducking instinctively as the silence was broken by a barrel crashing through a window quickly followed by an alarm ringing. Relieved, he realised it was far away and turned to run to the source of the sound. It was easy to pinpoint – three men were standing in the shards of their own carnage. One of them noticed Tommy's arrival.

"The fuck?" One of the looters pulling his hand out of the broken display window, holding a rations bar. "The fuck is this clown?" Snorting, the looter shook his head.

"You better put that back," Tommy announced as he approached. While it hadn't been the plan to pick on looters stealing food, he could not let that pass. He had a job... of sorts... to do.

"You really going to make me put it back?" The three men

walking up to him. The leader was pasty and sweaty, probably waiting for this all day since the meteor crashed.

"Everyone needs rations. No need to stockpile them." Tommy replied. Nearing the man, the smell of moonshine reeked on his breath. All alcohol on the planet was moonshine, but this was strong stuff. Watching as the leader started snorting, then spat at him.

"Go play somewhere else, kid." The man looked a bit jaundiced.

"You're sick. Aren't you?" He could tell now that he was a bit closer.

"Kid, you don't know shit." He scoffed, looking over, though there was more hesitation in his voice.

Grabbing the leader, he paused blinking. He could feel the man's vitals. "Your liver is about to give out on you. You put that food back, and I'll make sure you don't die in a month." He said, looking over him. He said it softly, giving the man the option to keep that information to himself.

The man's eyes bulged, and he nodded shakily. Tommy let the healing energy go through him, fixing the man's liver with relative ease. The man had to feel that it was working a lot better now. And hopefully, take that as a reason to drink less.

Dropping the rations packets to the floor, the man spoke to his men. "Let's go somewhere else. These are shit anyway." He started walking away as they hesitated.

Calamity at Cattori V

"Now!" He ordered, ignoring the looks his crew gave him.

"Nice display." Turning, Tommy saw a sandy-haired man hand-rolling a cigarette. Finishing, the man continued, "You got them to leave without any violence."

"I guess I did. What's it to you?" Tommy still felt a bit on edge after the confrontation, even though he was happy it had gone well. "I'm not up for games."

"No games. My name is Gorth." The shaggy man held up his hands, palm out, the lit cigarette in his left hand. "I think you've met one of my people...."

"Are you with the group V was telling me about? Because I'm not interested." Clambering down, considering, even if Gorth was with Violet? He would be careful just in case this Gorth was a CCC informant. he did not want to give up Violet's name, whoever she worked for? Somewhere he felt like she was a good person who was just trying to do what she thought was best to make this world a better place.

"I am," Gorth replied, taking a slow drag of the cigarette. "Has she told you about..."

"The wild conspiracy theory? Yes." Glad his scoff was hidden behind the mask because he was unable to keep a straight face. This Gorth looked unbelievably posh up close, with his groomed moustache and side combed hair. Even so, he had to be a criminal - he knew every free-born citizen of this planet around his own age or older.

Gorth took a deep breath. "I still think our side is where you belong."

"I disagree. There are no sides on this planet." And that, he felt, was the truth. The CCC was probably not the benevolent benefactor they thought they were themselves, but it was better than nothing. History lessons had shown them that life for the first people here had been excruciatingly hard. Now that the CCC was here, people could get jobs closer to what their actual skills had been on earth. That had to count for something?

"I still think you should see the work we're doing. We're not all bad." Gorth stated, tossing the butt of his cigarette to the floor.

"Uhuh. That's what everyone tells themselves. What are you here for, anyway?"

"Insurance fraud. But I really feel you should come with me before someone finds out your name." Gorth started rolling another cigarette.

Tommy paused. Violet had to have been the one who had told him his identity. She'd spent the night in his flat - not hard to find some letters or documents with his name on.

He relented. "I'll consider it."

A scream interrupted them, Tommy straightening up when he heard. Someone needed him more right now than some damn resistance leader trying to score a recruit. Tommy started running to the scream, glancing back just in time to see Gorth walking away towards an improvised pod waiting for him. The pod was of the kind Violet had used, saving him that first time. She wasn't at the wheel, though. Good, it was no kind of night for her to be out. He was sure she could handle herself, but at the same time, if she didn't need to take the risk, it was best to stay safe. There were many fewer women than men on the planet, and it meant nights like these, where chaos reigned, weren't safe for women. It was a dark reality, but it was their reality. The scream sounded again.

He ran into the night as fast as his non-motor assisted legs could carry him. This night wasn't over yet, and his charge was limited. As he approached the main street, he winced as he heard another window break and what seemed to be some furious yelling. Damn.

Chapter Twenty-One
Tommy meets Gorth

Waking up exhausted seemed to have become his default state of being—a loud announcement from the internal house comms waking him up.

Something had been very wrong yesterday. Not all of the looters had been human. Some of them had been Lhoorlian. Or had he imagined those tall feral forms walking through the streets with almost military precision?

There couldn't be enough Lhoorlians on the planet for him to even notice. It seemed impossible that he had actually seen aliens looters on this planet. Vivid memories of snarls and fights returned and made him shiver. He lost a few of these fights. He could tell from the pain and bruises.

Slowly he started waking up enough to listen to the announcements.

"Please report to your nearest factory for reassignment if you see an F in the top right corner of your screen. If you see an E, please report to the spaceport for further instructions."

"Please report to your closest Centauri Care Concern office as swiftly as possible if you see a C. This message will repeat in five seconds... Attention, Cattori Five is now under martial law. Any violent or aggressive behaviour will lead to incarceration or execution. Instructions to follow. Please report to your nearest factory..."

This was not good. Shivering at the thought of this planet under martial law. In all the time he had been here, he had never seen anything like that. Unplugging the helmet from its charger and pulling the suit out of the wash. Stowing it in his go bag along with some of his most prized possessions. If things were getting that bad, there was a chance he would not be coming back here. Glancing around the flat one last time before making his way down to the CCC building.

There was nothing left in there that couldn't be replaced. Materialism wasn't exactly encouraged here as it was hard enough to produce enough to go around. Let alone extra for some to be greedy about. Hopefully, Lion was at the CCC still by the time he got there. Rubbing a hand over his unshaven chin and sighing. Not a good look, but he had to make sure he was safe. As he walked down the street, a familiar pod design slowed down next to him, and a friendly voice came out.

"Oi, wonderboy. Get in," Violet called from a pod. "We're going."

Speak of the devil. He was just wondering if Violet was safe somewhere, hoping her group had made it to safety.

Glancing over, he replied, "I'm going to the CCC building, Violet."

Scoffing, she opened the door for him as the pod slowly rolled on at a walking pace. "To do what, Tommy? Sit there and do nothing while you could be much more useful out here?"

He stopped. She was right. Even though he had barely recovered from the night before, he wanted to help more than he had already. At the CCC headquarters, they would probably wait it out in relative safety and comfort. Why shouldn't he? He hadn't done anything wrong. He could use it.

Violet continued, "You're not wondering why there's a sudden martial law going on?" She gestured around at the people hurrying about. "Why are we just being herded now?"

"Maybe more meteors are coming. Maybe the big gas pipes were hit. Who knows! Not everything the CCC does is evil. Have you seen the number of looters around?"

She made a face again at him. "Fine. At least get in so I can stop yelling. I'll take you to their main building." She promised.

Tommy paused and licked his lips before she continued.

"Come on. It's like five miles with the tram out. If I can't convince you during this trip, I'll leave you be, forever." She promised, and he sighed.

"Fine. But only cause it's a ridiculously long walk." With a sigh, he got into the car. He wasn't sure why he even did. It wasn't like he would not have been able to finish the walk. In fact, he would have preferred it, considering he'd probably be spending a lot of time indoors, but something made him want to spend some time with her. If all this went very wrong, it was probably the last time he could spend time with her.

And maybe the cogs in his head had been turning since the night before. Perhaps it was because his mother was leaving the planet, something which had never happened before. Something was different about the whole situation.

The door of the pod closed, drowning out the street noise of the people outside. People running, grabbing stuff, trying to figure out where to go? While he felt he had the relative comfort of just... getting into a pod to enjoy a ride and some good company.

"So. What's on your mind?" Violet asked.

"Nothing much. Wait, is this Orchid's pod?" He looked around, his earlier suspicion confirmed. The smell was familiar.

Cackling, Violet replied, "I knew you'd notice! Not like on will mind. On's got like two of these. Not sure why, but hey! If you can get them." Shrugging, she reversed out of the busy main street and onto a quieter side street.

"You said we were heading to the CCC!" He protested, watching her leave the commotion of the metro area behind.

"And we will! But I just want you to know what we're all about. After that, it's up to you." Reassuring him with a pat on the leg.

"That's not what you said."

"I know, I lied. Get used to it." Clearly bored. "So how do you know Orchid?"

"How do you know Lion?" From the look on her face, he could see she had not expected that question, but he was going there. If Orchid with the CCC as he expected, the pod would not be listened into. Though on closer inspection, he could tell she had done... some work on the central console. The AI's hub inside the car had wires dangling from it. A hack job, but an effective one. It also meant she was entirely steering the pod, with no AI or autopilot to correct mistakes. Only the basic collision avoidance system's light seemed to be blinking. She had to be an experienced driver to pull that off. Maybe she was using her automotive knowledge from earth? Or had she learned it all here?

Finally, she sighed. "He's my brother. We pulled off the kidnapping together, though "pull off" is a relative term. He was the brains. I was the getaway driver."

"So you're Violet Lion." He blinked and sighed. "Great. I'm here with... Well. You both played me. Well done. Stop the car."

"Why would I? You'd be left further now than you were before," she added as she smoothly manoeuvred past a curve.

"Because maybe I don't want to be kidnapped?" He protested, holding onto one of the handholds inside the small cabin. Still feeling like he was too big for one of these damn things.

"That's kind of the definition of kidnapping, that you're not into it. Otherwise, it's just a kink. Devil's in the details."

"Tell me why I should listen to you after you deceived me like this."

"Because my brother is on the inside of that giant mess and hasn't contacted me since yesterday. That's not normal. If he's in trouble, I need you to find out, but you need to know about us first. Or you won't trust us."

"I don't trust you already, you crazy person. You just... pretty much... grabbed me off the street and... Watch out!" Tensing up as she swerved around another bend and narrowly avoided a set of recycling stands.

"You've met Gorth. He's our leader. We're a resistance movement who wants more transparency from the Centauri Care Concern. How much money they're making off us, if the government is aware, you know, the basics you would know if you were a prisoner on earth." She pushed down the speed pedal as soon as they had cleared the metro area.

"Fine! So take me to your fucking leader and see if I care. He's not going to change my mind because I'm not a criminal like you. I have nothing to fear from the CCC." Looking out the window, regretting this decision more and more as she drove away from familiar terrain.

"Fine, maybe you don't. Not yet. But with the city under martial law, the planet is under martial law. How long do you think that will take? Until you make a misstep and get a Warning?"

"I've already got one. It doesn't scare me. I'll get off this planet somehow." He was bubbling a bit now. He knew the whole Warning thing was already working against him.

"Wait, you have a Warning?" She looked over to him.

"Watch where you're driving!" The collision avoidance system started squeaking, and she turned the wheel without even taking her eyes off him. Her complete trust in the computer baffled him.

"Huh." She glanced back at the road, barely glancing at the obstacle she had just avoided. "So you do. Fancy that." He could see her pocketing a small communications device.

Taking in a deep breath. "At this point, I just hope I get to where you're taking me without you killing me first."

Calamity at Cattori V

"I'll manage." She winked and turned on the lights outside of the pod to see where they were going. "Don't worry, I won't let anything happen to you. My brother cares about you."

"That's nice," glancing over, he could see there was something she was leaving unsaid, and he didn't want to poke at it. Not right now.

They arrived at what looked to be a large cave. Tommy recognised it - he and his mum had come hiking here many times when they had lived in the city. They'd climb up the hills and picnic and admire the view. It seemed like it had been such a long time ago, now. A time where he thought this was a usual way to live.

"This way." She walked towards a bushy area next to the cave and brushed some of the bush aside. Similar to her wheel stash that first night. It moved with surprising ease to reveal a hatch with a combination lock. The beeping of the code made way for the soft brush of metal on metal as the hatch opened. Violet made her way in before whispering, "Come on." Following quickly, stooping to get through the low entrance.

"What is this place? Did you build it? I mean, the Resistance?" He had to remind himself it wasn't just her doing all this.

"No, it was a cave some of the pioneers lived in when they came. We just added some... security measures. Like a door." She added dryly.

"It works." Shrugging and following her in. After about ten meters of stooped walking, the cave widened, and small electric lights lit up the cavernous space. Drawings filled the cave walls, and lights had been draped carefully around the carvings he noticed with some surprise. That showed a respect for the pioneers he rarely saw.

"Now, the next part is annoying. It's a climb up the wall." She strapped her backpack on tighter, walking over to a wall with some carved out handholds.

"This place is... wow." Shaking his head in disbelief. Even if a CCC unit ever found it, it was perfect for holing up in. Anyone trying to get in would be trapped and slaughtered. The ridge up above had a picturesque view of the wider area, and as it was lit, there was nowhere to hide except the small tunnel.

Adjusting his backpack and starting the climb after her, and trying to control his breathing.

"Good hideout." His training with Orchid had helped his stamina a lot, but this was a steep climb.

"Thanks."

He was relieved to note she also sounded out of breath. When they finally reached the top, he pulled himself up and took a deep breath. "This better be worth it," he gasped.

A guy's voice answered, "I am sure it will be. Welcome, Tommy."

Calamity at Cattori V

Gorth walked over, smiling a little. Tommy nodded.

"Good set up you've got here."

"Still not sure it was a good idea to bring you here, but it's the best we've got." Gorth seemed resigned, walking to what looked to be a living area, set up behind a fence. Gorth continued, "Please come along. Would you like some tea?"

"Yes, that sounds great." Tommy had to admit - tea would warm his cold, stiff hands after that climb.

"Alright. Thank you, Violet. Go rest up." Gorth nodded to Violet, dismissing her. Violet hesitated but then nodded and walked off. She was treated with great respect here, which Tommy thought was a good start.

"Violet said you wanted to meet with me. Again." Remembering Gorth's introduction and recruitment talk from the night before. Tommy wasn't sure what either of them would be getting out of this now. Gorth continued.

"Yes. We do want to talk to you."

Tommy looked at Gorth, standing there by himself. He didn't see any others,

"And you are the resistance?" asked Tommy. What a day. This was never how he thought his life would turn out, but here he was. It felt like... his world view had been challenged. Curtains drawn. Peeking into his core, the essence of the planet working in a way the CCC could only approximate.

"So. What do you think is going on?" Gorth asked, and it surprised Tommy that he was interested in his opinion.

"I think..." He sighed. "A meteorite struck. There might be another one coming, so they want to put people somewhere safe. The factories..."

"Aren't exactly shelters. We've seen reports they are building things."

"You keep people busy, and they won't riot or panic. That's pretty much a given. Also, probably fixing things you guys sabotaged." He was baiting him with that, but the other remained placid.

"Yes... It is something this planet is prone to do, isn't it? Be kind." Gorth chuckled. "But if this planet was really kind, we would know everything there was to know."

Tommy frowned. Was this Gorth really that vain that he thought he should know everything? That nothing should be off-limits to him? He sighed.

"Maybe. But this is where we are. The CCC does a good job keeping tension low."

"Perhaps. But..." Gorth waved a hand. "I'd rather get to the point. We lost contact with Henry, and I'd like you to go in and check on him."

Tommy frowned, noticing the use of Lion's first name.

"Oh, no. You can't involve me in this." Panicking a little. If they caught him ferrying messages to Resistance fighters or whatever this was supposed to be...

Calamity at Cattori V

"Nothing serious. We just want to make sure he's okay. Go into the CCC. Violet will meet you at home tomorrow evening. They know you two..." Gorth shrugged. "If he's fine, there's nothing else for you to do. Even if he's not, we'll deal with it, and you don't need to do anything more. But neither Violet nor I can walk into the CCC building and just ask about Henry."

This was true. Tommy was in a good position, especially if it was just to check on his partner and friend. "What if they won't let me go home?"

"You're a resourceful young man, Tommy. I'm sure you'll find a way to help your friend if he needs the help." Gorth nodded. "Thank you. We all care for Henry."

Tommy suddenly realised why there was nobody here. It was so he couldn't compromise them even if he got caught. Shivering, he gave his answer with a sigh, "Yeah. I'd like to go now. I need to go in."

"I'll drive you."

Gorth was walking down towards the rim. He couldn't imagine the tall, elegant man rappelling down, but he made short work of the climb down.

Tommy shook his head, joined him, walked up to the ledge, and climbed down behind the man. He was glad to have solid ground under his feet again when he remembered the awkward tunnel.

"You guys sure have this spot secured," Tommy said, slipping out of the last bit of tunnel. It was a miracle his pants hadn't ripped.

"Thank you. We do try to keep this place safe and secure." Gorth added, casually wiping some dirt off of his pants and smiling over. There was a pod parked there, but it wasn't Orchid's pod from before.

"Who does that pod belong to?" Asked Tommy.

"Nobody who will miss it," promised Gorth shrugging and opening the door. "It'll be destroyed in a few days once it has served its purpose. A new one can be made."

Tommy shivered at the wastefulness of it, but it wasn't just that. Gorth's words showed such disregard for the class of people who could afford this kind of thing or had a license for it, at least.

"You dislike that?" Gorth questioned, glancing over as he opened the pod for Tommy.

"Of course, I do! It takes a lot of materials and labour to make one of these. Not to mention the waiting list for a new one is two years." Tommy shook his head and climbed into the pod. "It's just a waste."

"Don't get me wrong. Some of it will be recycled. But it's better to lose it than to risk the Resistance."

"See, this is what bothers me. You don't even know what you're resisting against. Sure, you'll tell me it's the transparency. But that's like cats wanting to know where the mice are hiding and demanding access to their holes. You just want to make things easier for yourself, not repent."

Gorth was getting into the vehicle with him. Gorth continued, starting the pod driving back into town.

"I don't think I'll be able to change your mind. But if that's what you want to think, that is your right. But just know we are doing what we are doing because we believe it's right. And after you let us know how Lion is, we won't bother you again."

Tommy suspected that was a lie. Gorth needed him to cooperate in this, so he would take anything said with a grain of salt.

Gorth took a turn into a backstreet to make sure they weren't spotted. It was a smart move, but it was still tense – there were a lot more guards running around the place. His worst fears came true moments later when a guard stopped them halfway to the main street. Gorth didn't even seem to flinch as he opened the pod door for the guard, smiling. The well-armed guard peeked in.

"License, sir?" He asked. Tommy tensed. This could end very badly, but Gorth still maintained his calm and merely reached into his pocket.

His mind racing also realised that if he just made a sound, a single word could indicate this man was the Resistance leader... He could bring the entire cell down. But that also included Lion and Violet. Letting out a breath as Gorth produced a very valid looking license. But it didn't have his name on it. The guard, a young man, immediately straightened up.

"Sir! I didn't recognise you. Sorry about that," the guard barked.

Tommy still saw him check the pod against the license as well. Smart kid.

"Not to worry. I recently had to change the photo on that license as well." Gorth grimaced. "We're not getting any younger."

The young guard chuckled nervously, handing back the license. "You have a safe trip, sir, remember curfew is still in effect, so please make sure to be in by dark."

"Will do. Just dropping my friend off near the CCC, so he doesn't have to walk." Gorth turned to Tommy for a moment, smiling, and Tommy was struck by the man's cocky and complete confidence in himself.

"Good idea, sir. It's not very safe out here." The guard closed the pod door, a sign of great respect, and waved them through.

Tommy sat back as the pod silently rolled into town. Looking out as the lights of the outside cascaded over them. Finally asking the question that was on his mind.

"You know, I wonder if anyone on this planet is who they pretend to be?"

Calamity at Cattori V

"Of course, they aren't. When you move someone an entire world over, they can become anyone."

"And who have you become?" Tommy asked, hoping to catch another glimpse of the license, but it had been tucked away already.

"A good friend to you and many on this planet," Gorth said. "And-"

"And if you're so chummy with the authorities, why don't you waltz into the CCC?" Tommy interrupted, having heard enough of his sweet talking and his bullshitting. If this man would ask him to risk his future, he wanted to know what he was about. What did Gorth actually stand for?

"This is why I had hoped we wouldn't run into a guard post. You're right. I have a standing in this society, but it doesn't allow me to go near the CCC. In fact, the opposite."

"So, who... are... you?" Tommy stressing every word, and Gorth stopped the pod. He feared he would have to walk the rest of the way, but Gorth merely pulled out the license and showed him.

The full name was Damon Gortherson. Clearly, the photo had been taken a few years ago, when he looked a little more relaxed and well-groomed. Not the strung-out version of him Tommy saw now. He looked away from the card when Gorth started speaking.

"I was the CEO of a major security firm on earth—one of the biggest. I went down for fraud, which cost many men their retirement plans, so they sent me here. I worried I'd get shanked in prison. So that's the irony. Many of the men here had worked for me before I was arrested, so they think highly of me. Tamara called me in on my first day and told me not to even come near a CCC office or building. We'd been competitors on earth, and she's still convinced all this is some sort of ploy by my company to get an edge on the planetary prison business. It's not. I fucked up. But people keep thinking I am capable, and that's how I started the Resistance." Gorth fired up the pod again and rushed it onward. "So that's my story. Believe it or not, it is of no consequence to me. But I've told you the truth now because I think your loyalty is the most valuable commodity on this planet right now."

"And you worry the CCC has my loyalty, so to speak?"

Gorth snorted, looking over, "You do work for them and are not very willing to betray them."

Tommy frowned, looking out the window before answering, "They're all I know and the only way I'll ever be able to get to earth. What you think of that doesn't really matter much to me. I'm just looking out for myself." His mother's words rang true in his mind. He could not get distracted by this planet.

"We're almost there."

For a moment, Tommy glanced over, pondering what he meant before he realised they were driving onto the CCC office's car park. Tommy grabbed his bag, "Thanks. Tell Violet thank you from me. Not sure why she cares so much about your stupid cause, but she does."

Gorth just sighed and didn't even protest his judgement. "If you can, let us know if Henry is okay."

Tommy paused. "What will you do if he's not?" He wondered, looking over to the other, waiting for his response. The lights inside the pod went out as the engine was turned off.

"Goodnight, Tommy."

Chapter Twenty-Two
Tommy goes to find Lion

Tommy walked into the CCC office with his backpack, mind racing. Gorth being unwilling to tell him what would happen if Lion was hurt worried him. The Resistance would be fine holed up in their cave, but waging a full-on assault on the CCC headquarters would be suicide. He shivered and looked away, heading for the receptionist in the main lobby, very much aware of the turrets mounted in the corners of the entrance hall. The office looked much the same on the ground floor, except that more guards had been posted.

"Hi." He rubbed his hands as he walked up to the man behind the desk, feeling himself warm up to the temperature indoors. "I was instructed to make my way here. Tommy Terrengan." It seemed the AI was offline, strange. Perhaps the computing power was needed elsewhere.

"Oh! Yes." The man tapping his name in. "You can head for the fourth floor, meeting room two, the one with the big screen. We're going to need you to help out, and it's very likely we'll need you to stay the night. Good thing you brought your stuff."

"Oh! That's just... my pyjamas." He fibbed, but the man was too busy to even notice. "So anything else?"

"We've had a storm warning, most likely due to the atmospheric disturbance of the meteor. We'll be lucky to dodge an impact winter..." The receptionist shivered. "Sorry! I'm usually in the meteorology department, but they asked me to take this station for a while."

"Well, I, for one, am glad to see a kind face rather than an AI." Winking, he wondered why the man would be here if they were worried about a storm. You'd want meteorology related hands on deck. He glanced up at the glass front of the office - the storm shutters were still tucked away, probably until the last possible moment.

"Thank you." Said the young weatherman, smiling a little. "It's a bit lonely down here, but I'm glad to be appreciated."

"You're welcome. Have a good night."

"Thanks." The receptionist took a deep breath and went back to scrolling. There was almost nobody here, so he didn't envy the man's position. At least it wasn't the outside, which was quickly darkening and growing colder. He looked around the deserted lobby and shook his head. It was usually so much busier than this felt otherworldly, eerie. He walked on.

An impact winter would be a catastrophe. Most of the

planet and its colonists were used to temperate climates, and houses weren't built for the cold. If the crop harvests failed, the reserves would be the only thing keeping people alive until help arrived from earth. That would take long enough for some to starve to death, easily. Walking up the stairs looking around for any signs of the AI listening activity, but it was all turned off. Even the lights were being replaced in favour of emergency lighting.

Not a great situation. The brutalist style building felt cold and threatening under the cold light, and he hastened his pace up the stairs. The emergency lighting gave just enough fluorescence to watch where you were going, but not much ambience. His echoing footsteps sounded loud and foreboding. His training with Orchid had paid off - he was barely out of breath by the time he hit the fourth floor.

While the stairwell had been doom and gloom, the fourth floor was light and warm. People were rushing about on carpeted floors with hot drinks and food. There was a particular loose atmosphere that never happened during workdays. From the smell of it, they'd been granted access to the holiday stores. Hot cocoa and fancy instant curries, morale-building treats, were being carried along into meeting rooms to groups of smiling faces. This felt more like a camp out than an emergency.

"Tommy! Hey!" Lion walked over to him, tie loosened, and his shirt was slightly undone at the top—a good look for him.

Calamity at Cattori V

"Lion! You're okay!" He put an arm around his friend and was happy to feel a hug in return.

"Yeah. I was here when... Well. I've been here most of today. It's been super busy." He explained, looking around.

"I'm in meeting room two, know what that's all about?"

Lion shook his head. "No. I'm in meeting room three. And I'm not sure I can say what we're working on."

The building was a sprawling structure. Meeting rooms two and three were not next to each other. Tommy frowned at that but didn't ask. "Yeah, seems like there's a lot going on." He kind of hoped Lion would volunteer more information, but it didn't come.

"Let me walk you to the meeting room," Lion offered after a moment of silence.

Tommy nodded and leaned closer. "Violet is worried. She'll be at mine tomorrow night."

Lion tensed. "I don't think we're going home any time soon, bro."

"Give her a call then. Just call my apartment." He said, sure she would spend the night there. It would be near impossible even for her to move in the dark in this chaos.

Lion gave a nearly imperceptible nod. "I think you guys are supporting the weather department with calculations. There's a lot of counting going on."

"Makes sense. I heard there's a chance of an impact winter."

"That would be the least of our worries." Lion said softly.

"What?" Tommy blinking and glanced over before stopping briefly.

"Tommy..." Lion sounded exasperated. Tommy could see it on his face, but it soon passed as Lion recomposed himself. "I just... I wanted to say... If I had had the opportunity, I totally would have gone for it. For you. You're handsome and kind, and I guess..."

Tommy tensed up as he listened. Did Lion just say what he thought he was saying?

"Lion..."

"No, shut up and listen. I like you, and if we survive this, I want to go on a date with you. Whether you screwed Violet or not. I want you."

Tommy felt his stomach do some bizarre things.

"I think I would like dinner with you." He admitted softly. It wasn't something he actively thought about on this planet. You had to watch your back. And if he did go to earth, there was no chance the other would follow.

"I like that. And... Just... wanted to tell you that." Lion leaned in and pecked his lips before opening the door to the meeting room for him.

Tommy nodded and walked in, still blushing at that interaction. The glass-walled meeting room apparently was not very soundproof. Inside, three of the meteorological department's girls were lined up, gawking at him coming in. One blew her nose loudly before popping a popcorn cluster into her mouth.

"Smooth shit man." Popcorn girl said.

Tommy groaned, looking around. "Hi. I'm Tommy. I was sent..."

"Yep, you are going to be our messenger boy." Popcorn girl got up. "I'm Monique. Please grab a seat. We're... We are working on some calculations. It would be handy if you could ferry them to the weather department up top. The internal comms are down, and these things are time-sensitive. You can also help us out by noting down the barometer readings every fifteen minutes." She pointed him at the barometer.

"But first, please, can you bring these up?" She handed him a thick folder.

"Meteorology is the top floor, just knock on James's door and hand these over. They're expecting them. Take the stairs just in case the elevator breaks."

Tommy nodded. It was clear they didn't really need him, but the CCC's orders to get everyone in here had led to an abundance of manpower. The women returned to their work, an efficient chain of calculations, checks and communication. He wished that he could be that useful right now, but he was just going to have to grin and bear it for now.

"Sure thing," he replied, but they had already stopped paying attention.

"Thank you," came the dismissive response from the nose blowing girl, more as an automatic response than anything else. Nodding again, he left the meeting room. Luckily, Lion had returned to his neck of the woods already and was not outside the door, probably involved in something much more interesting than meteorological calculations. Briefly wondering about Orchid. Was on in onis flat or in a bunker somewhere? On mentioned heading to the CCC on the last call.

The stairs were cold and dark as he navigated them up. Emergency power seemed to have been activated in the non-essential parts of the building. There was a window covered by the storm shutters every other floor, and he would glance out through it. Breathing evenly as he climbed the stairs, the last thing he remembered was taking a deep breath.

Suddenly a flash.

Before he could even realise what it was, he saw the explosion through the storm shutters, quickly followed by a smaller one. Ducking and screaming as the blast wave hit the tower. It seemed to last forever, but suddenly, it was quiet again.

Calamity at Cattori V

It was close, less than a kilometre away from the building. It had taken less than three seconds for the blastwave to hit. Letting out a whimper before straightening up again. The car park had now been razed by the blast. Hopefully, the storm shutters had taken most of the damage. The storm shuttered window now closed did not provide enough of a view to view the damage, but he could tell some apartment blocks had been annihilated. Their dark outlines, even though the tempered storm glass, were simply no longer there. He started running up the stairs to the top floor, almost falling out of the stairwell as he pushed the door open.

"There's been-"

"We felt it too, one of the women in the hall said, looking out of an unshuttered window. "That was not far at all. Luckily a lot of that area had been evacuated."

This did not feel like a meteor. This was a bombardment, and their location was being triangulated. The thought hit intensely and immediately. They were being lied to, the idea went round and round in his head. An office door had the name James on it. Stumbling in and handing over the file, and took a deep breath.

"I'll get back to my post," he felt the words shakily leave his lips.

"Alright, be careful." One of the scientists handed him a hand-cranked flashlight. "Just in case the power goes."

"Thanks." Smiling a little. His backpack was still in the downstairs lab, and a part of him was worried someone would root through it. Luckily it seemed everyone was much too busy with other things.

Heading out of the meeting room and back to the stairs, there was a building map. Trying to memorise it. Wondering briefly if his apartment building had held up? It would have been in the blast zone, with Violet inside. A pang of pain shot through him, not just at the possible loss of Violet but also the pain that would cause his friend. Rushing down three floors until he hit what had been designated as an off-limits executive floor. Shoulder first, he pushed against the door - luckily, unlocked. He guessed security was also considered non-essential as long as you monitored anyone coming inside.

After sliding inside, he closed the door silently. No alarms, no shouts of 'hey, you!'. A good start. The darkness was almost complete here. Taking out the flashlight and shining it through slits in his fingers.

After a moment to gauge whether the layout matched up with the map he had memorised, he walked on. It seemed deserted - nobody else was here as far as he could hear. Every muscle in his body felt tense as he continued to shuffle through the hallway. Right now, he really, really wished he'd brought the backpack. The helmet had some excellent night vision.

Suddenly, he could see a door handle reflecting the light of his torch. It hadn't been on the map... so an excellent place to start looking for the truth. He tried the handle, and his luck continued - it opened up easily for him. He smiled a little to himself and slid in, making sure to close the door quietly. So far, he'd been fortunate, and he hoped it would last. It was bright and loud all of a sudden.

His eyes needed to get used to the light briefly, but when he did, he took a moment to look around. It was daytime. Nothing had happened. He was standing at the edge of a city square that looked similar to the one near the headquarters, except that the flowers, the trees... they were different—other colours and shapes. People walked around, wearing a very different fashion, and talking in all sorts of languages. Cattori Five only had Terran, and while he heard a lot of that, there were other languages as well.

What was this? Had he gone through a portal? He whipped around, but the door was gone - there was just a bush in its place. He rushed towards it, but he felt nothing. Starting to panic now. Running through the square, trying to find some way of getting out, or waking up, whichever was the most applicable. He couldn't have just... He ran. A sudden loud beeping and a mass of people waited to cross what looked to be a busy road. He was being pushed around. That drove him over the edge. He screamed, and the lights went out. He felt his body crumple to the floor.

Maybe he had fainted? No, there was another sound now.

"Tommy?" A familiar voice. Tamara Cattori walked over, and he shivered, unable to get up just yet.

"What was that..." His overwhelmed senses were still trying to cope.

"An earth simulation," she remarked, looking over him. "Hard light figures and a plan adapted to familiar geography. It's a model we use to get people like you used to the idea of earth."

"People like me... What?"

"Get up." Tamara turned around, and the lights came on gradually.

The whole place looked like a giant plateau. The ceiling filled with projectors, lights and speakers far above, hidden behind a glass dome that had probably produced the illusion of a sky just moments earlier. He was guided to the edge, Tamara showing him a ladder. As he made his way off of the plateau via a ladder, Lion walked over.

"You always end up where you don't belong, don't you just?" Lion was shaking his head, looking up at Tamara climbing down. "We should cut him loose."

"Now now. You know just as well as I do, we were going to involve him at some point." She stated, pulling out a chair. Below the plateau, a large table had been set up with a multitude of computer terminals, probably to control the projection. Which was likely where the power had been diverted to.

"So why this... projection?" Tommy asked, looking back up.

"As I said, rehabilitation. Not just for people who've never been to earth, but also people like your mother who haven't been there in a long time."

She explained, looking over at Tommy. There had been nobody besides him up there. "But... who was it running for then?"

"You activated it stepping on. It was designed to react to you and a small group of others. Had we not been near, it would have still been running." Tamara said.

"What is going on?" He demanded. "Outside. We're not being pelted by space rocks. Someone is attacking. That's why you got everyone sheltered. Isn't it?" He pushed. His heart was still racing after all this, and his tone was perhaps a bit too acrid, but he wanted to know.

Unfortunately, before she could reply, there was another bright flash through the storm shutters.

Chapter Twenty-Three
Tommy Catches Up

"That's definitely not meteors." This time, Tommy felt safe to probe a little more. Maybe it was because of his experiences since his first meeting with her. Maybe it was just this situation.

"No." Lion admitted.

"And I'm sorry but who are you?" Tommy snapped. This man was meant to be his coworker. His friend. And he'd had some very mixed interactions with him. A chat, a leg healed. A chance that he was a double agent, a kiss. Him knowing Orchid.

"Gorth told you, huh?" Lion sighed. "Yeah. I'm with the resistance."

"Does-"

"I know, but it does not matter right now!" Tamara sighed, rubbing her face. "We need him. We need a lot of people we'd rather not need right now."

Tommy sighed, heart racing in his chest still. Not just from the simulation but also from confronting the other.

Tommy gasped as Violet limped in ten minutes after. At first, he didn't recognise her – she was covered in dust, blood and soot. Clearly not the work of an asteroid.

"They're coming." That was all she said. Lion grabbed her and pulled her close, and she closed her eyes. Tamara straightened up before saying.

"We can fend off an attack. Sure, not the best time for it, but this place was designed to withstand prisoner riots. The shutters alone can keep them out."

Tamara walked to a terminal and checked it, Tommy noticing a smile when she looked at the screen, flashing a big 304.

"Who is attacking us?" Tommy screeched out. Nobody had really taken the time to explain anything to him.

"Lhoorl." Tamara said casually. "Lhoorl has been attacking us. Get Orchid."

"Lhoorl?" He repeated, disbelieving it.

"Yes. They asserted we trespassed in their planetary domain, whatever that means. We were given an ultimatum – vacate the planet or be annihilated."

"So the rehabilitations..."

"It is an evacuation, yes. We hoped we'd have more time, but half the planet's workforce is building ships. In less than twenty-four hours, we would have been ready to go." She said, taking a deep breath as Orchid walked in from the other room.

"They're no longer responding," Orchid said.

"The ultimatum only ends in two days. Their goal is to rattle us." On said.

"You've been talking to them?" His head was booming from the explosion and all that was going on here.

"Orchid has been interpreting for us. They were quite... sure we would understand their language, so we lost about a day trying to find anyone to translate, which led to their first attack. If Orchid is right and they mean to rattle us, they won't make a real attempt at the building." She licked her lips.

Self-confidence was not really radiating off her, but Tommy wanted to believe her. Their best chance was to get off of this planet before they did start attacking in earnest.

"So, what's the plan?" Violet was glancing over while wiping her face clean with a cloth Lion had grabbed for her.

Tamara answered, "We sit it out for now. Not much we can do. The planet is in lockdown, so any ground troops can do little damage." Large calibre gunfire roared. Everyone could hear the sound of rapid-fire artillery guns coming up through the many floors. It vibrated even the thick stone.

Calamity at Cattori V

"You guys have guns?" Violet asked, mood seeming to lift a bit. She had wiped the soot and dirt off of her face.

"Be kind, but be prepared," smirked Tamara.

Orchid walked into the room, nodding, "They will be unarmed. Lhoorlians consider it dishonourable to fight with weapons."

"Easy for them. They're beasts." Lion added, sighing. "I will happily fight with dishonour."

"Same," Tommy added, glancing over Violet's injuries asking, "May I?" Seeing Violet nodding, he continued, "This will hurt." He pulled her arm, popping the arm back into her socket with a simple twist and snap.

"What w- AAAH! Fuck you!" She screamed before calming down and saying in an exhausted voice, "Thank you."

Glancing over her body, he'd healed most of her cuts and bruises before the arm he had popped back in started healing.

"You're welcome. How's your ankle?"

"Painful, but it's keeping me awake, so I don't mind." She laughed. "That's not a bad thing at this point, I guess."

"Need me to-"

"Nope, nope. You save that magic juice. Just in case." Laughing, she seemed almost exhilarated now, possibly the endorphins kicking in.

"Thank you for that," Lion thanked him while taking his

sister's hand and smiling before reassuring them both, "We'll live through this."

Briefly remembering the turrets downstairs. Again, the night reminded him of that night long ago in his mum's house, which had almost been looted. In many ways, he was in a better position than back then. He glanced around. Everyone looked afraid. But the desperation he had seen in the faces of his elders many years earlier was missing.

The downstairs barrage slowed – the gunfire became shorter, more sporadic. Every time there was a noise through the building, things seemed to grow tense, but nothing happened. Everyone stayed put. Some even managed to drift off to sleep.

Chapter Twenty-Four
Plans are Formed

It grew cold and dark on the executive floor. It was hard to see one another with the single camping lamp on the table, lighting the room as dimly with its small ring of LEDs. Tamara sent a guard to get her a blanket. Lion and Violet had snuggled up together. When he tried to move closer to Orchid for warmth, though, on growled in a way that Tommy hadn't heard since the Lhoorlian attack. Even if the fighter was not a biological Lhoorlian, it sounded quite scary, and he decided to keep his distance. And even when sleep came, it was fitful and restless.

Finally, Lion piped up. "Orchid, you've fought in a Lhoorlian war. What was it like?"

"Hell." The dull reply came. "The war broke out when I was a child and didn't let up. I was taken in by the anarchist tribes. They have the right idea. Burn it all down and start anew. What else can we do at this point?"

Tamara snorted, "Attack another planet. This is probably doing more for planetary peace than anything your emperor can come up with."

"True," Orchid admitted. "I wouldn't be surprised if they hyped up humanity to be some sort of enemy of the Lhoorlian people, an imminent threat that needs to be taken out immediately."

Tommy broke in, "So, what about the Lhoorlian that was transported here?"

"He was an informant. We found him, lost in space," said Tamara, hardly looking up from what she was doing. Her conscience was clearly not muddled by any of this.

"Lost in space or ejected into it? Big difference." Orchid asked dully.

"Ejected," Tamara replied. "Our message probe picked him up and brought him on board the transport ship. We were hoping to get information about them, but he turned out to be less than appreciative."

"You interfered with Lhoorl business." Orchid looked over. "What did you think would happen?"

"We didn't even know it was Lhoorl business. We thought we were rescuing a shipwreck survivor, didn't even know whether he was alive. He..." She sighed.

Confused, Tommy had to ask, "But that wasn't what started the war, was it? Was it? You said..."

"No, we're in their space," said Tamara dully. "We're evacuating as fast as we can. Earth probably only just got the news about what is happening here. So it's the fate of an entire planet on my shoulders. I take that seriously."

Tommy felt bad for her for a moment, then realised she had gotten very rich because of this planet. Suddenly, that empathy melted a bit.

Turning to Orchid, Tommy continued, "Tell me more about this whole Lhoorlian war thing. You were with the anarchists?"

"In peacetime, there were three factions," started Orchid. "The imperialists, the ruling family and his followers. They believe the planet should be ruled by an emperor and his court so everyone else can just spend their time on research and science and more fun things than politics."

"Lhoorl does that kind of thing?" Lion asked, and Orchid shot him a glare.

"We have spaceships, don't we?" Orchid replied acridly. "And a very advanced sense of both geology and meteorology."

"What about the other parties?"

"Second biggest are the demarchists. Literally, a group of people who want to complicate everything and use a lottery to decide who rules for the next ten years, then switch it all up again. To keep that going, they'd divide the planet into smaller regions and go with that, but that's... Not something everyone agrees with. Mostly it's people who want more say in how the planet is run, but how can you even get that when the lottery decides who wins? Oh, and lastly, there are the anarchists. I'm not sure they're even a party as they're hostile to both the other parties. They want to tear down everything and rebuild from scratch. When the war started, they vowed to do just that, and it's working out pretty well for them."

"Last I heard, it really was just between the imperialists and the anarchists."

Tommy shivered. None of this was very good, and it didn't seem like there was an easy way to resolve any of it.

After a moment's pause, Lion asked another question to the room, "So how many can we get off the planet?"

"In two days? Not enough," Tamara answered, rubbing her temples. "And earth won't be happy about a bunch of exiled people being returned, but even if they could, they are unable to help us. I can't let people be slaughtered. Criminals or not."

"Gee, thanks." Lion made a face at her. "So glad the supreme ruler of our happiness wants us to live."

"You can shut your mouth, Henry. You and your entire Resistance have been sabotaging factories. If people die because ships aren't ready in time, that's on you."

"But... What if the Resistance can help?" Violet sat up. "We have caves. Weapons. We could hide. If this is just a temporary distraction to them, we can hide a few years, decades, and emerge when all is calm. They're not interested in this planet, or they would have tried to colonise it already. Or just come while we were not here. This is just a show of force."

Orchid nodded. "She's right. They didn't see humans as a threat before all of this, so it would have been a cinch to just send some colonisation machines here. The humans would have gotten the message in the end."

Tamara nodded. "If they can produce their own ships to escape when the time is right..." She licked her lips. "I'll need to check resources, but this option, using the resistance caves, that could save some lives."

Tommy nodded and sat closer to Lion, leaning against him.

"Just for warmth." He said softly.

Lion chuckled. "Don't mind either way," he said simply.

"Counts as a date?"

"No way Jose. You're cooking me pancakes."

Through the shutters, the light started to filter through.

"We made it," whispered Violet.

"Live to fight another day." Orchid chuckled mirthlessly. "Get up." On opened the shutters.

"They left their stuff behind," said Violet as she stood up and joined Orchid at the window. "Or... Oh." She blinked, shocked at what she saw outside the windows. Tommy stood up and saw the bodies on the floor below.

Tamara called to the men around her. "Their stuff can be helpful. Grab what you can and scout for their landing ships. The more tech, the more ships."

"Go!" She ordered the guards. Nobody seemed to believe they were still alive, but once Tommy made it downstairs, he could see why. Only about six soldiers were lying by the building. They had really just been trying to rattle them.

Tamara put a hand on Tommy's shoulder. "You. How did you do that with..." She looked around to Violet.

"Can't say," shrugging the arm off and walking towards the stairs. "I just can."

He needed his backpack – he really didn't want to leave it on its own much longer. Through the night, he'd been afraid of it being stolen.

"But you're the vigilante." Tamara walked after him. "The Angel, or whatever they nickname you."

"I'm just a guy, ma'am," he answered, shrugging. "I don't know what you want me to say."

"Nothing, actually. We need to keep the peace. If the people knew their Angel was allied with the Concern...."

Whipping around, he let out his anger, "Let me get one thing straight. I'm not allied with you. Not with the Resistance. You can all go to hell. I want to get to earth, and if I can help some people, so be it. But I'm not some organisation's lapdog."

She stayed quiet. "Are you done? Good. However you want to define yourself, remember which camp can get you to earth."

Calamity at Cattori V

She turned around to go speak to a group of guards.

Hissing and walking away from her, he grabbed his bag and headed towards the building's exit.

"They sure did some damage." Lion glanced around, with Violet already clambering onto the vehicles the aliens had left by the entrance.

"But not much more," said Tommy, looking around. "Most of that was because of the bombardment. So... What's next?" glancing at Lion.

"I'm going to speak to the resistance," said Lion. "You should get to the spaceport." He looked at Tommy. "If... If your mum survived, her ship is leaving in a few hours."

Nodding, he did want to see her again. He really did hope she had made it. But even if that chance was slight, there was little else he could do right now.

"Thanks." Gathering up his things, looking around the miserable little group of people. None of them seemed to have gotten any sleep. And somehow, they were all in this together.

Putting his backpack on his back properly and starting the walk to the spaceport. This time the PA systems were quiet, not wishing anyone a good day. *Too bad*, Tommy thought. *We could really use it right now.*

Chapter Twenty-Five
The Goodbye

Tommy arrived at the spaceport two hours after he had set off from the CCC building. It had been a long walk, and he hadn't slept very much, but it was good exercise. As long as he walked, he didn't have to think about what was happening to the planet. The attacks from the night before. The fact Orchid was a force for good in this ridiculous setup, despite being the closest person to a Lhoorlian on the planet. His run-in with Gorth and their conversation.

Hopefully, Lion could convince them of the half baked plan they had for all of this. Despite last night's chaos, it was a beautiful day. The sun was up, and it was warm, delightfully so. The sky was clear. A perfect day for a spaceship to take off. The spaceport was so familiar, but only the arrivals hall. He'd hardly ever been to the departures, and he needed a few minutes to find it, arriving just in time to see the pods with the old farmers arrive. They all dismounted, carrying very little of their possessions with them.

Calamity at Cattori V

Seeing him, Chrissy perked up and waved. "Son! Oh gosh, you look a mess. Did you sleep at all?" She was clearly surprised to see him.

Making his way over with a smile, "Hey mum. So glad you made it. And no. Not much. With all that was going on...."

"Like some meteor storm was going to stop us. A group of kind strangers showed us a cave to shelter in." She smiled, though there was something in that smile he knew—her devious nature.

"The... resistance?" He asked softly.

"I guess so," she waved a hand, mainly towards the one yawny guard that was following them. "They were very nice to us." She concluded. Nodding, he left it at that.

"Well, I'm glad you're here." He hugged her, thinking with a twinge of regret it might really be the last time. The ship could be attacked and crash. Perhaps he wouldn't make it.

She hugged him but then let go. "Remember what I said. Don't stop remembering it until you board a ship just like that," nodding towards the waiting Infinity ship.

"I won't, mum. Promise. I think it won't be very long." From what he had understood, they would be evacuated. The whole process of applying for earth permits would be suspended. Probably only until he actually got to earth, but even so, there wouldn't really be anywhere else he could go.

Shaking her head, she said sadly, "I can't believe we're actually going. It'll be such a waste of the nice lavender on the field."

"Mum. Trust me. Going to earth is a good thing. Do you know where you'll be settling?"

"I've barely had the time to think! They told me it's the south of the United States, Paneurope was also very popular, but I want somewhere warm so I can grow my lavender... Also, I don't think my old bones can stand the cold much longer."

Chuckling at her answer, he offered some encouragement, "You're stronger than you think, so I'm sure you'll make it work." He kissed her forehead.

"Come see me, okay?" She looked up, tears in her eyes. She had moved away from him when he was ready to live on his own, but... this was different.

"I promise I will." He guessed she had no idea it might only be a few days before he would be on a ship as well. Once the evacuations ramped up, they would have to rush them.

"Okay," she said, taking a deep breath and dabbing her eyes with her sleeve. "I'll send the CCC word of my location so they can pass it on to you."

Hugging her again, "Just use my work email. It should still work. You should get on the ship. You don't want to miss it."

She laughed. "I guess I wouldn't, but I'll be stuck in that tin can for so long." She looked around and over the field. "I'm scared. Earth will not be as kind to me as this place was."

"This place isn't kind, mum. You just made it kind." He squeezed her hand and looked around to the stairs to board the spaceship. Her companions had already made their way up. Not many people here had families.

"I was just lucky to have a son like you." Chrissy smiled and squeezed his hand back before stepping onto the ship.

Tommy watched her until the doors closed, and an announcement was made to clear the field, at which point he walked to the observation deck. He was the only one to watch them until the ship cleared the sky. No fire, no explosions. It cleared the sky easily to head for earth. Another ship was being wheeled out, and soon another pod with people would roll up. Perhaps thinking they were the only ones leaving. With only a few passengers per ship, they would have to have back to back take-offs to even get a percentage of the population off the planet.

He was just glad they'd been allowed to leave, though he guessed that was what the Lhoorlians wanted. Any incoming ships with people on it, especially soldiers, would probably be targeted.

The roar of a pod startled him, and he looked down from the observation deck to see Orchid's black pod. Sighing, he made his way down as the pink-haired one opened the door, getting out. Orchid stood statuesque next to the shining pod. On had clearly showered, and the lack of sleep was much less clearly visible on Orchid's chiselled features than on his own.

Orchid greeted him, "Thought you might need a ride back."

"Thanks. We uh, we need to talk to the resistance."

Orchid nodded. "Violet and Lion are already on their way there. Want to stop there as well?" On sat back down in the pod.

Tommy joined him, glad the pod's seats were more spacious than that of the CCC's duty pods. Settling into the designer seat and strapping himself in before leaning back.

"I think we'll have a better shot, all four of us talking to them."

"You're an optimist," snorted Orchid, looking over. "Anyway." On strapped onself in and then started the pod. Turning away from the spaceport, on asked, "So, you saw someone off?"

"My mother. She's been rehabbed. Though we both know she's been evacuated. I guess they sent her first cause she's so low risk at her age."

Orchid nodded. "You should be on a ship out yourself."

"I can still be of use here!" Bristled Tommy, turning to him.

Calamity at Cattori V

"Not saying you're not." Orchid turned around to on. "But I'm just saying. Your powers would be useful on earth. You could do a lot of good."

"I could," he shrugged. "But right now, I feel like it's needed here most of all."

Orchid peered around, making a turn before Tommy realised.

"Wait a second, how do you even know where they are hiding?" He asked, seeing Orchid steer without hesitation. Even he didn't know that well.

"I know things, Tommy. That's what I do. Also, they tried to take me, so of course, I'm going to try and find them first."

Tommy blanched, looking over. "You mean that night, with all the men..."

"Yeah. I think I punched your boyfriend's lights out," on simply said.

"He's not my boyfriend," Tommy protested, closing his eyes for a moment before looking questioningly at Orchid. "But why would they?"

"As far as I know, at that point, they just saw me as working for the CCC, and that was enough. Now hopefully, they can stop seeing the CCC as the bad guys and play nice for a change."

Sitting back into his seat and staring up, Tommy added, "I hope so too."

They reached the cave not too long after. It looked a bit of a shambles - people were clearing debris from the entrance, and Gorth's pod was gone, though Tommy guessed he might have gone ahead with his plan to destroy it. Violet was there looking up from her work and waving at Tommy. She hesitated when she saw Orchid. "Why's on here?"

"Hey, Violet. On gave me a lift."

Grinning, Orchid said, "What, you guys wanted to take me not that long ago, and now I'm not allowed to visit? I'm appalled."

"So, anyway," Tommy interjected, "We were hoping this would convince Gorth to switch teams and help us out."

"Gorth's dead," she said softly. "He ran his pod out to draw fire away from the cave. It worked, but he didn't come back." She looked into the cave, shaking her head, "Everyone's pretty upset..."

"I'm sorry to hear that," Tommy replied. "He cared a lot for you guys. I know that much."

"Thank you. Oh, come in." She gestured towards the cave. "We had a partial cave in and are still clearing some of the rubble to keep the opening as clear as possible."

In case of another attack, and we have to all flee, thought Tommy. He nodded while looking up and around.

"It still looks pretty stable." At least it did up until the point where they had to crawl.

It still felt a bit claustrophobic, probably because this time there was less urgency, so more time to think. Scurrying through and breathing a sigh of relief as they came out the other side.

"How many people are here?" Orchid wondered.

Violet answered, "We have around fifty to a hundred people. Only Gorth really knew all the details," She licked her lips, "There are cells spread around." With a sigh, she started on the climb up the wall and Tommy followed her.

He tried to talk as he climbed, "Does - ugh." But it was pretty exerting, and even Orchid wasn't mouthy as they scaled the wall.

Once up, he looked around. Two or three people were being bandaged, and he resisted the immediate urge to run over and heal them. Minor injuries were best left to heal on their own, so he could save his strength.

"So uh, this is the big headquarters?" Orchid looked around, unimpressed.

Violet bite back, "Yeah. You can stop smirking. We're doing all we can."

"No, no. I was just amused that your group thought they could come take me down so easily." Orchid shrugged.

Tommy couldn't believe it. At first, he had thought Orchid was just cocky, but there was actual ability beneath all that. Not exactly the world's most congenial, but Orchid knew onis own strengths and limits, which was what made on formidable in any kind of battle. He could learn so much from Orchid, but their paths would separate soon if all went well. What also worried him was the fact that if everyone was brought to earth, that would include the likes of Orchid. Orchid would not thrive on earth. This war zone was where on was in onis element and where on would perform best. On earth, on would be a dangerous maniac who would probably end up in prison. Or executed. How could a government excuse a murderer even if they had helped save a planet?

He shivered at that thought. How many of the people currently being considered for evacuation would be alright? Brought back to a planet where there was no crime because everyone who committed anything worse than a misdemeanour could be shipped here? Or maybe earth would be a lot worse than here?

Violet prodded him, whispering, "What are you thinking about?"

Chuckling nervously, he lied, "Nothing."

"Alright." She was nodding and seemed satisfied.

He noticed Lion looking over before announcing, "I guess I'm in charge of this lot now. I'll round them all up, and we can discuss our options."

Tommy nodded in agreement. Lion looked just as tired as he felt.

"Maybe we should get some sleep first," whispered Tommy.

Calamity at Cattori V

"Nah. We don't have time to waste. We only have a little over a day left. There isn't much we can do."

"Dying of lack of sleep is one of them," Violet said dryly. "Three hours. Go sleep, both of you."

Orchid simply gave them a nod. "I'll keep an eye out until the morning." On promised.

Tommy sighed. "Fine. Is there a bunk somewhere?"

"Of course. I'll show you," Lion said, walking over to another stone edge climbing it. After a small, easy climb, they came to a warmer part of the cave, where blankets and pillows were laid out in piles next to folded mattresses.

Lion led the way in, grabbing a mattress and laying it out with some blankets and a pillow, so Tommy followed his lead. The fatigue was really starting to hit him now, and he fell asleep as soon as he had kicked his shoes off.

Chapter Twenty-Six
The Lhoorlian in the Cave

Without an alarm clock or sunlight, Tommy slept longer than he expected. When he did finally wake, he felt a lot better. There was a pang of guilt seeing Lion was already up, though he had not stowed the sleeping materials. Hopefully, that was because he thought they might spend another night and not because there had been an emergency.

Though in about a day, none of it might matter. The timescales were not in their favour. Rolling out of bed, putting his shoes back on, climbing down from the sleeping shelf. He wasn't sure if it was the cave or the last few days, but he would have given an arm for a shower. As soon as he hit the central area, Lion looked up at him.

"Hey!" Lion smiled a little, "There's some food if you want it."

"I do. Where is everyone?" He did not see anyone from the resistance.

Lion sighed as he shook some ramen into a pan. "They've gone into hiding in other caves or to help build. Without Gorth, there's not one single person they listen to, so I let them make their own choice."

Tommy sighed. Great, just what they needed, more free agents roaming around.

"You're worried," Lion stated as the ramen cooked.

"Yeah. It's a big mess out there, and to have people just wander about or not know where they should be... scares me. It's easier to end everything on this planet if there's chaos."

"Starting to sound like Tamara there," Lion was shaking his head and dropping another brick of noodles into the pan before mixing in the sauce powder and stirring it in. Tommy saw him wipe his hands, then forage the fridge for extra ingredients.

He couldn't remember the last time anyone had cooked for him. Clearing his throat, he asked, "So, what's next?"

"Violet's ferrying everything that's useful here to CCC headquarters, including Orchid. We'll need to help defend it while they're evacuating." Lion cracked a few eggs into the broth, and now Tommy could feel his hunger growing. How could simple ramen become one of the most desirable things? Lion added some spices, a handful of mangetout peas and stirred.

"Smells great."

"My turn to cook for you, after all." Looking over his shoulder Lion smiled and shrugged. "Jeeze, luckily they have showers at the CCC."

Tommy laughed. "That bad, huh?" Running his hand over his chin, he definitely felt stubble there. He didn't even want to try and sniff his armpit. Felt like two weeks had passed since that moment only a day ago where he had been called to the CCC and the first meteor strike, which he now knew hadn't been one. His world had literally changed overnight, and it freaked him out. So far, there had been very little time to stop and think, so he hadn't had much time to process.

Lion carrying over a bowl of ramen, with some sesame seeds sprinkled on top.

"Thank you," Tommy said, sitting himself down onto the floor and taking a bite. "Gosh, this is pretty good for cave cooking."

"It's the cooking I do the most." He laughed and looked over. "I barely cook in everyday life."

Tommy chuckled. "Yeah. But this is good nevertheless," Slurping in another spoonful, the hot broth tasting like the best thing ever. It had been a while since he'd had food, after all. And in the cold of the cave, it warmed his bones right through. Wondering how the meteorology girls were doing with their popcorn and tissues. If they still thought a meteor had struck and been still working on their calculations. Or if they were dead.

Calamity at Cattori V

No, the building had been safe. There should have been no casualties besides the guards in the lobby. He took a deep breath and looked away.

"So we're going to the CCC?" Tommy asked between slurps of hot ramen.

Lion sighed and looked over before answering, "Yeah. I wouldn't have thought so myself, but it's the best place to be for now."

"I know, world upside down right?"

It was the first time they were genuinely alone since Lion had told him about his feelings for him and the kiss. It made him a little nervous. He hadn't had the time to process any of this, let alone his emotions, and it felt like he should say something, but he couldn't.

"Someone's coming," Lion said, putting his bowl down and walking to the edge, hissing when he looked at the weapons cabinet, it was nearly empty. Tommy slurped in the last mouthful, regretting that he would have to put the food down.

"Are you expecting anyone?" He whispered. There was a definite sound of shuffling coming from below, and he could hear pebbles toppling.

"No, and this does not sound like anyone who would know his way around here." Lion said, grabbing the last weapon, something that looked like a stun gun.

Tommy walked to the edge with him to peer over. He saw a single Lhoorlian soldier dragging himself into the cave. The alien was clearly distressed. A straggler who got separated from the group, Tommy guessed. Dangerous, but clearly injured. The soldier dragged his wounded leg, slowly seeking shelter from the sun outside. Lion's breathing did not quicken, though it sounded loud against the quiet cave. Glancing over, he could see Lion just aiming the stun gun down at the man. The projectile would easily hit at this distance, so Lion just took the time to aim properly.

The Lhoorlian, perhaps sensing something was wrong, glanced up and snarled, a row of white, fang-like teeth baring easily. Lion took the shot. The alien dodged it easily, moving the moment he had spotted the two of them. Smart, thought Tommy, which he didn't like. Especially as the alien started climbing the wall. The strong claws found easy purchase on the roughly hewn walls. Tommy dived for his backpack, pulling on the top and pants as fast as he could, adding the helmet last. If that thing was coming up, he wanted to be ready for him.

Lion nodded at him encouragingly. "Does that have weapons?"

"Not really, but it is protection!" He said, putting the helmet on. "Is that stun thing all we've got?"

"Fraid so," said Lion, grabbing a new charge for it and then turning to fill a jug with some of the boiling water from the cooker. "Time to get creative."

Stepping forward, holding the jug over the edge, Lion tipped the water down onto the climbing Lhoorlian, who screeched as the boiling hot water cascaded all over him. Tommy glanced over – he had lost his footing for a bit and fallen down about five foot. Still, the being quickly regained that distance and started clambering up again.

"I think you just made him mad." Tommy swallowed.

"Any better ideas?" asked Lion, backing away. The alien reaching a clawed hand over the edge. Tommy walked forward, stomping his booted foot on it. Hardly a heroic thing, but the best he could come up with. Despite a loud yelp, the alien held on, twisting and grabbing his ankle.

"Oh, shit," Tommy tried to back away, but he had a hold of him and had found enough of a foothold to launch himself up.

Tommy could see Lion jump forward to shoot a stun bullet into the alien from the sidelines, but it barely fazed the alien. Trying to jump back so the alien would be forced to let go, but the spindly form just came along and landed on top of him. The alien put clawed hands around his neck and started choking him. Tommy was pinned. Kicking at the alien but the weight was too much. Recognizing the armour, the alien snarled and redoubled his efforts to kill Tommy, leaning in and hissing. He could smell the acrid breath waft out the alien's mouth. Hoping he smelled at least as horrible to him as well. He raised one hand to stun the creature with his taser, the enraged soldier barely noticed the electric current.

Running up with the hot pan from the stove, Lion smacked the being in the face. The alien hissed loudly, letting go of his throat long enough for Tommy to punch out and wiggle himself from under the thing's form. The alien was breathing hard, but he was hardly even bloodied. The skin was bright red from the burns they had caused him, and it had definitely made him angrier. Remembering what Orchid had told him, he cried out, "We gotta go! There's no way we can kill it!" Lhoorlians were nearly impossible to kill. Especially with their improvised weapons.

Lion called back, "If we climb down, we'll be trapped! That thing could just nail us while we climb. We need to somehow incapacitate him!"

Tommy looked around for a weapon. The alien was scrambling for something as well, and Tommy just hoped Lion would get to it first.

Tommy set himself up between Lion and the alien and grabbed him by the shoulder, dropping to the ground and rolling down. He was on the floor again, but this time he had control, at least some. Wincing as he landed on a bad patch and turned, the alien was on the bottom, Tommy straddling him. His fists pounded into the alien's face, and he kept going until he stopped moving. With a soft whimper, he got up and staggered back.

"Tommy!" Lion's voice cut through the haze of adrenalin. "Are you okay?"

Blinking a few times to calm himself, and nodded. "Yes. Yes, I am." He sighed and hunkered down onto the floor with a cold shiver. "Fuck. He's not dead, is he?"

"No, I can see his chest move. But I think the cave is his now." Lion shoved some stuff into a backpack and then strapped it on before starting the climb down. Tommy grabbed whatever looked useful, shoved it into his own bag and then started down. Granted, Lion had left very little but a few packs of noodles and some flares, but you never knew when you could use a snack and a bit of fireworks. He climbed down quickly. He was getting the hang of this cave wall climbing now that he had had to do it a few times.

Tommy squinted into the bright outside. Glaring light made such a difference from the inside of the cave mouth, looking around to find Lion. Driving up on a makeshift vehicle, probably left by Violet, Lion gestured at him, "Get in!" He paused, "Or on. Not quite sure." The four-wheeled vehicle had two seats, a wheel in the middle and a canvas canopy, which would keep the sun off them. Clambering on clumsily and settling in behind Lion, bracing just in time to before Lion sped off. The alien had not peeked out of the cave yet, but he understood why it was best to put some distance between them.

Lion leaned back before saying, "Jeeze. There could be more. I don't know how many landed."

"Not to mention the ones that seemed dead and were just wounded. They'll have healed up by now." Closing his eyes, trying to recall everything he could from what Orchid had told him. It had never been their main topic, but he had wondered about the aliens. Just hadn't imagined such an up-close and personal meeting.

"They can do that?" Lion gasped. "Fuck. Fuuuck."

"Yeah... They are very sturdy, hard to kill. Nothing much phases them. They regenerate faster eating meat and... well, we're just prey. They're not taking prisoners unless it's their own kind... Ugh. Orchid told me so much, and I can barely remember it!" He knocked his head against the headrest and sighed. "How is Violet so good at making these things?" The engine under their butts was puffing away, roaring once in a while as Lion hit the gas.

"She's just good at mechanical stuff. On earth..." Lion's voice died as he shook away the thought before continuing. "Think we'll make it there?"

"I hope so. This place isn't going to be the greatest to live in in a few days."

Chapter Twenty-Seven
Back to the CCC

By the time they reached the CCC, the improvised vehicle was starting to fall apart a bit. It had made a valiant effort, but once the resin had started melting under the heat of the sun, there had been no hope. As they tried to park next to the building, the axle broke, and they had to abandon it.

Lion, laughing, looked over the vehicle. "Damn. Would have been fun to drive that thing around a bit longer."

Tommy laughed with him, checking the area. The dead had been cleared - but he wondered by whom? There had been dead alien soldiers here this morning, so it was very likely the aliens had picked up their dead during the day's cease-fire.

"Yeah. Let's go inside." He shook his head. The damage was still pretty extensive, and to see the usually pristine city in such ruin... He sighed. Maybe they would rebuild, but then he remembered it was much more likely the planet would just be abandoned. Overhead, he saw another spaceship take off.

He wondered how Earth would deal with the influx of people? If they would all make it back safely? There was so much that could go wrong. He shook his head and walked into the building. This time there was no receptionist, and Tommy just hoped he was okay. Maybe he was just getting some sleep somewhere?

That fleeting suspicion was confirmed when the man suddenly shot up from behind the desk, looking a lot less clean and proper than the night before.

"Oh. Hi, Tommy Terrengan, Henry Lion, right?" Looking over his printed list. "Yes. Top floor, Miss Cattori is expecting you. At sundown, we're expecting more attacks, so the storm shutters will be closed as soon as the sun starts setting."

He ran a hand through his hair. "We've got ammunition for the turrets, so we're not expecting too much difficulty if the numbers we encounter are similar to that of yesterday."

Tommy nodded at his optimism, but there wasn't much conviction in the man's voice. They were all tired after the first onslaught, and the second one would be coming soon. And after that... They would be free sport to the Lhoorlians coming down.

"Take the stairs. The power has been cutting out from time to time." The receptionist added from behind the desk, looking over his tabletop.

Calamity at Cattori V

"Alright!" Tommy sighed and put a hand up. He did not look forward to doing all the stairs up, and from the looks of it, Lion was willing to risk being stuck in an elevator. But after a moment, they both headed for the stairwell.

The building was cold and only the daylight coming in from outside helped them find their way. Repeatedly, Tommy glanced out the windows. The higher they got, the more of a view he got of the city, and it broke his heart to see. His apartment building was completely gone. It was lucky Violet had survived that.

"What's on your mind?" Lion asked, only slightly out of breath as they hit the eighth floor.

"Just how many lives must have been lost and how lucky we are."

"Ironically, their deaths may help us." Lion said, grabbing the handrail and looking back over the burnt city.

"How so?"

"Because if we all had made it back, earth could easily have told us we're overreacting, that there was no real danger and possibly send us back. Now that there's casualties, they can't dismiss us so quickly."

"Tamara did mention that she had told Earth about the danger. How long does it take for a message to get to earth anyway?"

"Not as long as a shuttle, but still. It just means they know we're coming. They can't send us anyone to help. This planet is doomed, and now all we can do is grab as many survivors as we can and get off."

Tommy sighed. "The people who hide..."

"Honestly, I don't have high hopes for them. Maybe. It's the best chance for people who aren't on a ship when time runs out, but it doesn't mean I'll like it." He looked away with a sigh.

Tommy nodded. This place wasn't made for a mass evacuation and the number of people they would save... It probably wouldn't be enough. The people remaining, if they lived and the Lhoorlians left them alone, would have to start over again like the Pioneers had at one point. They wouldn't have a clean slate to start from, though, and the best bet they would have was to turn the farms into their home field and grow as much food as possible there. Anything beyond the essential nutrients would be a luxury for a long time.

He might be here for all of that. He had no illusions that he was low-priority when it came to being moved off-planet. In fact, he had no real idea in what way Cattori and her board had organised the evacuation. However, it had seemed they had evacuated the elders and low-risk criminals first. At least his mother wouldn't have to see her farm destroyed.

Calamity at Cattori V

Briefly, Tommy wondered why the Atlantans weren't stepping up. Did the frail aliens fear the Lhoorlians, or was it up to them to fix everything? Was that why he had been given his powers? If so, why hadn't they just warned them of the impending danger? Or had they, but had he missed the signs? He shook his head.

He took a deep breath and looked up. Three more floors. And again, they were alone. At some point, the kiss would come up, and he wasn't sure if he was ready to deal with that. He kept his head down.

"What's it like? Earth, I mean?" He asked, remembering the simulation.

"It's... loud and busy." Lion sighed. "But it's also a lot bigger, so you can get away from it as well." Lion smiled a little. "There are some farms as well, so it's not all city."

"I saw the simulation. It's so busy." Pausing as he tackled the next set of stairs.

"It can be in the big cities. I came from one of the big cities, and it was a lot sometimes. But it gets easier. You get used to it."

"Okay. I think, if I do make it off, I'd like to live on a farm." He smiled a little at that idea.

"You will make it off. I promise." Lion smiled back, "And that's a good idea. It'll be quiet, and you'll be able to get used to things. It's also cold. The seasons are very different from here. It can get really cold. We're almost there." Lion was properly out of breath now, probably because they'd been having a conversation. He merely nodded and made his way up, slowing down a bit. Tommy caught up, stumbling the last few steps before sitting down.

"Give me a moment here," Tommy said, letting out a breath and putting down his backpack. "Phew! I just don't want to roll in there sweating and puffing."

"Yeah," Lion sat down next to him and peered out the window at the remains of the city. "Think it'll all get destroyed?"

"What a waste that would be. I mean... hope not. It may be. But I suspect they'll just try and scare us off and then... go back to their own crap. They're still at war on their own planet after all." Tommy finished, standing up, "Let's go in. It's cold here."

"Yeah." Lion nodded and glanced out the window a bit longer before getting up. Tommy was so relieved the subject of the kiss wasn't coming up again. At least for now.

Violet looked up as the two of them entered the room.

"You made it!" She exclaimed, rushing up to hug them both, then raising an eyebrow. "You look and smell like shit."

"The cave was attacked," explained Lion by way of apology, "by a Lhoorlian. We barely made it out."

"Shit!" Violet swore, putting a hand to her face. "Did you kill it?"

"I think we just made it angry to be honest," Tommy explained, "but we knocked it out long enough to get here. Thanks for the ride you left."

"You're welcome! See, brother, it's nice to be appreciated."

Lion chuckled. "The weapons?"

"Orchid took most of them," Violet said gravely. "We ended up needing them. Whatever hadn't been killed came back in full force." She sighed and shivered at the thought. "Don't piss that one off."

"I know." Tommy said, "On taught me how to fight. I heard the Resistance scattered. I'm sorry."

"Don't be," Violet answered, shaking her head. "I know we're all just trying to survive, and honestly. There's not much we can do."

He could tell she was torn up about it. The situation wasn't simple - fleeing or hiding, and for most of these people, there wouldn't be enough ships to take them to earth. He shook his head briefly.

"Alright. What's the plan here?" Tommy asked. The top floor was at least warm and lit for the moment. Violet then explained it all.

"Tamara is coordinating the last few ship builds. What she's told me is most ships come with a bunch of spare parts to survive the journey, so ever since she found out about the threat, she's been asking for and collecting more of the extra parts. We're looking at making a few new ships with them. They'll be cramped unibody things, but they last."

Planet factories would be more than up for building the ship's hull, as long as there was an engine to take the ship into orbit. Even as a lifeboat, left to be picked up by other ships, it was better than being down here when the Lhoorlies landed in full force.

Then Tamara arrived. Walking in, she said in clipped tones, "Just in time. Come on."

She strode back through to the large emptied out floor. The screens showed other building levels, factories where space ships were being built, and more monitors hanging from cabling and struts coming from the ceiling. Plans for small spacecraft were scattered about the floor, and Tommy felt his heart sink. This was such an improvised mess, grasping at straws on a planetary level. Pushing people off the planet in the spaceship equivalent of a rubber dinghy. They would never make it, but if he even voiced that, all hope would be lost, and he couldn't do that to any of them. At that moment, he realised they were all just hanging on to something to do.

Orchid made onis way over. "I contacted my people on Lhoorl." On cleared onis throat, "Well. Not my people. But once they find that out, there's going to be little they can do. The imperialists are not interested in causing loss of human life if only because that means they'll need to do more clean up." On sighed. "They have agreed to give us three ships. They should hold six hundred total. But they do consider us taking that offer as our unconditional surrender. As soon as the ships land, they disembark, and we get on or are executed."

"I have... so many questions," Tamara said in drawn-out frustration. "If they are willing, can't they just call the entire thing off?"

"The most influential group on the planet is still the demarchists. They are leading this attack. The only reason any party is willing to help us is because they fear the demarchists plan to use the planet to drop off their enemies once they win. Nobody wants to deal with angry natives. No offence."

"None taken. I'm not a native." Lion chuckling, glancing at Tommy, who just rolled his eyes.

Tamara looked up from her calculations. "Six hundred on the Lhoorlian ships plus the ones we are building here... We may just make it." There was hope in her voice.

"What about the people in the prisons?" Tommy asked.

She raised an eyebrow, "Oh! You mean the super-secret prisons nobody has ever seen. Nobody has ever seen or escaped? Yeah. Those aren't real." She shook her head.

"What?" Violet exclaimed, flabbergasted.

"There are no secret prisons—too much work. You forget the CCC has a skeleton crew down here. Not much more." She shook her head. "The rumours were doing wonders for peace, though. It was pretty good."

Tommy sighed. He should have guessed when even he had never seen the damn prisons.

Violet chuckled good-naturedly, "I guess you do have a point." Looking back to the monitors, she asked, "Can I go down there? I'd love to see if I can help out in any way. I have an engineering background."

"Wouldn't have guessed from the vehicles you've been leaving all around town ever since you got here." Tamara reached into a locked drawer and handed her a badge.

"Here you go. There might be a stickler down there insisting on these, so take one just in case. Though I doubt anyone still cares."

As if participating in the little charade, Violet clipped the badge onto her shirt and nodded.

"You'll need to grab the elevators down. The stairs won't go far enough. Take the stairs down to ground level and ask Giovanni to activate the elevator down to the labs for you."

Violet sighed. "Right. Let me go kick some engineers. I'll see you when I'm done down there!" She waved and headed for the stairs.

Tommy called after her, "Just be careful not to overdo it with the arm! So... what do we do?"

Tamara looked at him, "Until night falls, we don't expect we'll need much. You could get some sleep or grab some time on the Earth simulator." She nodded to the platform. "It might be good for when you get to Earth."

Nodding, the idea of spending some time in that simulator wasn't too bad, actually. Looking up at it, feeling nervous, Tommy could feel himself tensing up.

"You may need a guide." Lion said, smiling, "Can I join?"

"Sure!" Tommy agreed before even realising. But having a friendly face with him would help a lot. And someone who could put things into perspective, as well.

"If you'd like... We could make it a date?" Suggested Lion, looking suddenly much younger than his age.

Tommy thought it over a moment. They had little more than a day left, one night, and then until the next day's nightfall.

"Yeah. I'd like that."

He finally decided, holding an arm out. "No promises. But I'd love to spend my last few hours just... doing fun things. We'll probably still see a lot of battle."

Lion nodded, taking his arm. They both knew it was very likely the Lhoorlian armies would send some more troops down to rattle them and that the ones who were down there, healing from last night's attack, would probably join their forces.

Tamara pushed a few buttons. "You get one hour, then you should get some sleep. You both look like utter shit." She muttered, shaking her head before she launched the illusion.

Chapter Twenty-Eight
Time Spent in an Illusion

This time, the effect wasn't as jarring as before. Maybe this time, his brain knew that it was entering an illusion. The sound was gradually ramped instead of just becoming an attack on his senses. Entering the platform, buildings grew around them as if cupping them into the illusion. The smell is what threw him - despite the overwhelming feeling he was outdoors, he could smell the insides of the building still.

"So...Earth really looks like this?" Tommy asked, peering around.

It looked like a park area, a grassy area bordering ringed with a tiny stone wall. The round patch of grass had four benches on the sides, pointing inwards at the minor pathways cutting through. A few trees were planted outside the small wall, blocking out the street noise a little. There was the sound of chatter, people talking and laughing, and clicking of shoes on the pavement.

Definitely a better scenario than the one he had walked into previously. A few others were sitting around, reading books or checking small devices that looked like phones. Still, he guessed they were just holograms from the fact they were wearing different clothing. Oh, and the fact that they weren't freaking out about an alien invasion. That bit as well.

"Some of Earth looks like this." Lion nodded, "There are parks like this all over. We usually just... go to them to relax during the day or to socialise." Lion looked around, summing it all up, comparing, "This one's rather small, like you would find in the centre of a city. It's probably based on a European one, based on the size." Chuckling, "Everything's smaller in Europe."

Taking it all in. From the grass to the sky and all the small details. Feeling like just ripping loose from Lion and running around to explore everything, but he had to take it slow. He did not want to risk the same sense of overwhelming dread that had gripped him when he had been here before, unprepared. He gripped Lion's arm, and he let him. Tommy thought of something to ask, "How far does this extend, you think?"

"Probably far enough that we could make it to that coffee shop." Lion took a step forward, and they were actually moving. Even though he knew they were on a stationary platform, it fooled Tommy for a second.

Lion tried to explain, "Moving multidirectional mats. It's... like a treadmill, except we can actually go places on it. You'll feel it bounce just a bit under your feet because it's basically a layer of rubber."

"Jeeze, they really thought of everything. I wonder where all the money for this came from?"

"From us, of course. Our work, our exports, everything that is okay to go to earth is sold and made into profit for the company." Lion sounded a bit bitter, and Tommy remembered the Resistance's ideals.

They had been lied to and things hidden from them, but it was not as bad as any of them had thought. Whether that made it better or worse, he couldn't tell. But it definitely made a difference to them both, in different ways.

"You haven't told me what a coffee shop is yet." Tommy changing the subject, joking he said, "I'm guessing it has some sort of coffee?"

"Ahem, yes." Lion laughing, "Have you ever been on a date before?"

"Not as such. I mean. Plenty of hookups." Romance wasn't really a thing on this planet. Everything was too pragmatic. Kind, but practical. There was no such thing as dating or courting here, just fulfilling basic needs.

Lion explained, "Well, on earth people go on dates." Shaking his head, "This is so strange."

"How so?" After the last twenty-four hours, nothing seemed strange anymore.

"On earth, we also have movies about space and all that. One of the tropes in such movies is human men showing aliens ahem, how they make love on your world." Lion laughed a little. "This feels kind of like that."

"Except I'm not an alien. I'm human." Tommy looked into Lion's eyes, laughing, "Just a cultural alien. Tell me more about the date thing, though."

Lion stumbled as he pushed on before saying, "Ah, yes. You ask someone if they want to go for a drink, or coffee, or dinner. And then you talk while having said beverage or meal, and you get to know one another. It's become a kind of thing where both parties dress up for it to show their best sides only," he said, opening the shop door and holding it open for Tommy. "There's a lot of ritual around it. What to order, whether to drink, who pays, opening the door for the other, all of that. But I don't think we need to worry too much about such minutiae."

Feeling laughter in his voice, he commented, "Sounds like a plan."

Tommy entered the shop instantly feeling surprised by the cosiness of it. The shop was about the size of his apartment, with maybe five tables scattered around and with a bar at the end with big boards above it. The thought that all of this was just an illusion never fully left his mind, but it was so convincing. His tired brain just wanted to stop thinking. Part of him just wanted to get this over with and go and sleep, but the other part of him felt that somehow, this was important. This was his life, after all. It could end tomorrow, and he would rather do something new with it.

Lion asked, "You're still sure about this?" It looked like Lion had picked up on his hesitation, so he nodded.

"Yeah. I am," laughing a little, "I'm tired, I'm nervous, but I want to do this."

"Alright. Just a date. Nothing more." Lion was reading the signs above the counter. Tommy could almost imagine the smell of coffee.

The drinks on the list looked alien, strange.

Wondering aloud, he asked, "Think the drinks are real?"

"Not sure." Loin walked over to the barista, who handed him three cups of coffee on a platter, appearing from seemingly nowhere. "Oh. I think I found a glitch." Lion laughing walked over to a table regardless.

He had to admit to feeling curious, "It smells like coffee."

"Yeah," Lion made a face, "but it smells like Cattori Five coffee. On earth.... Coffee is much better. We make it with a blend of two beans, arabica and Robusta. Robusta is the less tasty kind, but it gives the coffee a great smell. Arabica is the good stuff, but it's more expensive. So we mix them to get the best blend. But here, it's all Robusta because it's all we managed to grow." He laughed. "So it's really only good for espressos and lattes and anything you can add a lot of other things to."

Tommy smiled. He was learning a lot just from this, and he could tell Lion was glad for the distraction as well. "Didn't know that. I just generally liked the tea better."

"Oh, it's way better here!" agreed Lion. "I never had tea on earth, but here's it's the best. I'm sure I'll miss it."

"Maybe we can stash a few kilos onto the ship. I mean, I bet this stuff sells on earth as well, so we can just use it to start over." Tommy chuckled at thoughts of tea smuggling. It couldn't be hard to find a few bricks of tea and stash them with his outfit.

"Good idea, though I'd be too tempted to have them myself." Lion waved away the thought, "Anyway. Date. We talk about ourselves. Those are the rules." Again, that slightly awkward, nervous stumble like when they had met. That seemed so long ago now, even if it had been less than a month.

"Yeah. I mean. So." Tommy sighed. "What did you do before you got into trouble?"

"Oh! I was a detective. A little bit like what we're doing here but... You know, different." Lion shook his head.

"So different how?" Tommy asked, sipping the coffee, it was suitably disappointing, but he wanted to keep up the charade. Adding a few spoons of sugar, wondering if it really was sugar or just an illusion as well. He guessed he would just have to give the coffee another try.

Another side effect was that he had no idea about the passage of time. This whole place seemed to be still, never changing, and he guessed it wasn't exactly made for using more than an hour at a time. Still, he was having an okay time. A bit of escapism in this crazy time. It was nice.

"Well. I was working for the law and not some private company, so that's the main thing. On earth, the structure is very... different. There are many more layers than here, and it'll be hard to figure things out, but I know you'll learn. Besides, you won't have to go to jail like some of us." He laughed. "From space prison to spaceship to prison again..."

Tommy groaned. There it went again. The conversation again shifted to everything he wanted to avoid.

"Okay, can we not talk about aliens or spaceships or planetary disasters for ten minutes? You know what. Tell me about you." Feeling his patience with this was wearing thin. He didn't like this whole game of pretend. He didn't like that they were here when the rest were working on getting out, and even here, they couldn't shut up about the situation.

Lion sighed deeply after a pause.

"I'm sorry. It's just... very on the forefront of my brain, I have to admit. So, you'll just have the government, and there's the police working for the government, but without the bit where they make profit. And we have stuff like Scoldings and Warnings, but it's much more... formal." Lion looked frustrated as he tried to explain, failing a little, but Tommy still enjoyed it. Part of him really looked forward to Earth, and he hoped somehow he'd still be able to spend time with Lion. Maybe not romantically, but definitely as friends.

Tommy nodded, admitting to himself, "It sounds complicated."

"It is. I guess you've been lucky with the simplicity of life here. I hope you do well on Earth, Tommy."

Tommy blinked at that. "Why are you saying that like we'll never see one another again?"

"We may get separated on the way there." Lion offered, but he could sense there was more to his words.

"So? Then you'd come find me. Jeeze," shaking his head. "You're my friend, and I will come find you."

"Tommy, I will probably go back to jail. You're free. It will be an adjustment, sure, but you're innocent, so you'll have your freedom to do whatever you want. I won't. The government will have to decide what happens to people like us."

Sighing, it was dumb, but it had never occurred to him that even after all of this, his friend was still a criminal serving time on this planet. Alien attacks should at least merit a reduction in a sentence. He felt so.

Lion grinned and looked over before optimistically adding, "Anyway. I served some of my time here, so it shouldn't be much longer." He paused, glancing around, "That isn't right..."

"What?" Tommy looked around. Something was off, but he couldn't put the finger on what it was exactly.

"They're all looking at us," whispered Lion. "I haven't been in many of these, but I'm pretty sure that's not how it's meant to be."

The chatter around them had stopped, and all the holographic figures had indeed turned to them. The barista reached under the counter for something and took out a long broomstick, wielding it with both hands.

"That's definitely not meant to be," Tommy said as the figure approached.

Grinning, Lion said, "I think it's time we skip right to the end of this date and possible kissing." Lion got up, looking around at them, "Follow me."

There was a low roar from outside the simulation as the shutters slammed closed, a noise he remembered from yesterday. This was definitely not normal, as far as he could tell, it wasn't dark yet.

Lion grabbed his hand, and they started running towards the exit of the illusion, a large hallway that leads to the stairs down.

"They can't hurt us, can they?"

"They can definitely touch us, and if you can touch hard enough, that would definitely hurt," Lion surmised. "Either way, do you wanna spend more time here?"

"Not really!" Following towards the end of the illusion's reach. It was only a few metres ahead until he realised they were making no progress towards it whatsoever.

Then realising their mistake, looking at each other, they both said it.

"The treadmill."

They had barely made it out of the coffee shop, and now they seemed to be stuck in the middle of the simulation, nowhere to run.

"Shut it down!" Lion called out, hoping the people below would hear. It was a far cry considering how far up they were, but it was better than nothing.

"What's the top speed of the treadmill?" asked Tommy. "I wonder if we can outrun it."

"Not a chance, this thing is mechanically sound with many a safeguard, but without it... If we go too fast, we may break it."

"Breaking it might not be the worst option." Tommy feinted one way but then u-turned the other way, and the carpet had trouble keeping up for less than a second. Then it caught up with him, but Tommy was still running. Lion was not too far behind and tried to keep up the pace.

"Just keep running." Tommy sped up and noticed this time the treadmill made an audible whir noise trying to keep up.

"What are you doing?!" Lion sounded out of breath, but they just needed to keep the sprint up.

"Keep going!" This time he found it hard to speak as well, as he was getting exhausted. His legs ached, the dull thudding on the treadmill harder than expected. It was designed for walking.

"We're going the wrong way!" Said Lion, and Tommy was well aware. They were almost out of the square now. The slow-moving NPCs had nearly caught up, faces serene and quiet. Eery.

"Trust me!" Tommy called out. "Stop!"

He dropped to the floor. At the top speed of the carpet, they were almost catapulted towards the other edge. As soon as it came into view, Tommy grabbed for the handrail of the edge. The simulation had figured it out now and reversed fast enough for him to feel his arm being pulled, almost out of his socket. He clenched another arm around the balustrade and pulled.

Lion clenched his hands around his ankle, determined to stay there. The treadmill's movement was like sandpaper being rubbed over them, and instinctively, Tommy kept his face away from it as much as possible. His pulling paid off as Lion grabbed the balustrade, and he managed to heave his own body onto the stairs, falling down them.

"Lion!" Sitting up and trying to get up, his body still disoriented from the quick changes in movement. Lion's face popped up, clinging to the balustrade. A moment of relief on the man's face, but then the metal bar cracked and gave way, and he was dragged out of view.

"No!" Tommy rushing down the stairs, pushing buttons to stop the simulation, but it stayed online. "Tamara!

Orchid! We need to shut the simulation down. It's gone rogue!" But he couldn't see them. With the storm shutters down, the only illumination came from the simulation up above. He could barely see anything.

"You are enemies of the Lhoorlian empire and should be destroyed." A computerised voice sounded before repeating it in Lhoorlian. Tommy shivered.

"Orchid! Tamara!" Crying out again, ignoring the computer. He had no idea what was happening, and it didn't sound like his AI Belinda, either. More like... something deeper and more savage. Either way, he didn't like it one bit. And he had to shut the simulation down before the worst of the worst could happen to Lion. Even if that meant shutting down the entire building's AI.

"Tommy! We're here!" Tamara called back at last. "Violet is shutting down the Cerebellum. It just went rogue all of a sudden."

"I noticed," Tommy remarked dryly. "We need to shut the simulation down. Lion is stuck, and the NPCs are hostile!"

"Working on it!" Violet's voice sounded over the radio. "Ma'am. I'm going to need your override codes."

"I can't give them to a convicted criminal!" Tamara sounded appalled.

"Not much of a choice unless you want to be stuck in here," Violet told her in a crackling radio voice. "Hurry! This thing is armed, remember? It controls the turrets in the hallway, and we have people inside!"

Tommy shivered. They had been designed for outside threats, but they could easily take out people too close to the exit. Hopefully, the receptionist fellow had taken cover when all this started. Maliciously, it had started slowly, luring them into a false sense of security until it was almost too late and the shutters had slid down around them.

Tamara glanced around before sighing, her shoulders slumping. "Alpha. Four. Nine. Seven. Tango. Victor. Charlie. Nine again. Two. Zero. Zero. Plus sign. Three."

A long pause followed, and Tommy worried the AI had found a way to block the radio waves. Suddenly the emergency light flickered on with a soft buzz.

"Cerebellum disabled. I'm checking Belinda as we'll need some AI to run the turrets and shutters." Violet said.

"I don't even want to know how you know so much about this building." Groaned Tamara, "But yes, please. It will be dark in one hour." The monitors showing the outside turned on, but Tommy wasn't watching them.

He ran up the stairs, looking around over the now dark platform. It was hard to see anything with emergency lighting. It wasn't designed to illuminate the platform. Maybe it was a later addition? The need had not been foreseen for this area. He reached into his backpack and slipped on his gloves, which had LED torches on the glove backs. Turning them on and sweeping the beams around, looking for his friend. A coughing noise. Tommy sprinted towards it, finding Lion curled up, trying to sit up. The harsh light probably didn't help, but Lion looked horrid. His nose appeared broken, and his eyes were swelling up. Coughing, Lion brought up some blood. Tommy dropped down beside him, looking over the damage.

"Looks bad. Let me heal your nose, so you don't get more blood in your mouth." He licked his lips and put both his hands on the man's cheeks, directing the energy into them. He closed his eyes as he focussed.

Suddenly, he felt lips brush his own and then go in for a deeper kiss.

It felt nice. He enjoyed it a second before backing up.

"Guess you're feeling better, then?"

"Still feeling kinda horrid, but I'll feel better getting off this infernal plateau. What happened?"

"The AI went rogue. That's all I know, at least." Sighing and looking around, he decided to head for the stairs, using the beams for light and picking up his backpack where he had dropped it. The stairs were tricky in the dark, especially helping Lion, but they made their way down without further injuries.

"How are you?" Lion asked him as they walked over to the two others.

Tommy sighed, "Rattled. Exhausted. Not much more that can go wrong is there?" He chuckled bitterly. Tamara looked up from her computer console as they came close.

"Good news and bad news."

"What's the bad?" Lion asked flatly. "I just had my nose broken by a fucking AI. Just give me the bad stuff first."

"Cerebellum went rogue. It somehow turned against us."

Tommy added, "I heard it speak Lhoorlian. Did the aliens hack it? Also, the whole bit of us being enemies of the Lhoorlian people..."

It was then Tommy noticed Orchid in the room. On was scoffing, "That's... such a ridiculous thought. First of all, the computer architecture is much too different. It wouldn't work even if we tried. Secondly, Lhoorlians don't use weapons. Even using your own AI against you would be considered use of weapons."

"It isn't just an AI. It's a supercomputer." Tamara said prickly. "I don't know. Its wires must have gotten crossed."

"Definitely." Tommy ridiculed.

"I do know," Orchid said. "The phrase "enemies of the Lhoorlian people" hasn't been used in forever as most Lhoorlians don't consider themselves one people anymore. It must have picked it up from some ancient propaganda."

Lion scratching the back of his neck, added, "Conveniently for the Lhoorlians. I don't like this one bit. No, sir."

"The good news," Tamara sighed, "is that Belinda can take over the turrets at least."

Tommy sighed. "Oh, thank goodness she can do something useful for a change."

"I heard that," said a familiar computerised female voice in somewhat sulky tones, "That's a Scolding, Tommy. Consider yourself warned about the use of foul and degrading language."

"I'm sorry, Belinda. We're all a bit on edge." He did mean it. He did not want to cause the computer keeping them safe any upset. "So anyway. Thank you for womaning the turrets and keeping an eye out."

"You're welcome." Belinda seemed placated, "Gosh, looks like my resources are so spread out that that Scolding never made it into your file. How about that."

Tommy chortled, doubting it would make a difference even if the file was updated. There was no way that data would make it off the planet either way and if it did, it probably wouldn't mean much to Earth that he'd been a bit snippy to an AI once.

"Thank you again, Belinda. What's the situation outside?"

"Ships are appearing quickly. Some are landing just outside of the city. Others are orbiting just outside the planet's atmosphere."

Lion turned one of the screens, "Don't need an AI to tell you that." The screen showed ships heading towards them. "I'm guessing a lot of them are headed here. What does the loss of Cerebellum mean for the shipbuilding?" Lion asked. The AI had been working on that kind of thing for the last while, along with its human workers.

"It'll definitely slow us down." Tamara sighed, "No offence, but Belinda is a social AI. Even with some of Cerebellum's resources, she's stretched out. Violet. Can you assign more of Cerebellum's cores to Belinda?"

"Negative." came the radio response, "They've been burned out, short-circuited or just plain on fire." Sounds of a fire extinguisher hissing came over the radio, "Fire's out, but there's not much left, I'm afraid."

"Alright. Belinda, please focus as much as possible on defence and assign any extra resources to shipbuilding. Human comfort is secondary."

"Copy that," Belinda acknowledged the order. "A change of pace! This is so exciting!"

Tommy briefly felt for the AI. Soon all humans here would be gone, and it would be alone, guarding empty buildings. Or would it learn Lhoorlian like its predecessor? The AIs had thinking processes that were very different from those of humans. Perhaps Cerebellum's betrayal had made sense to it, considering the number of aliens heading down to attack the planet.

Tommy took a seat and sighed as he looked over everyone in the room. It was a pretty dim mood. It was less than an hour now before they expected the aliens to attack. The closer it came to the countdown, the more brutal they would get.

"Proximity alert!" Belinda boomed. "A group of aliens is approaching the building." The cameras switched to a small group of Lhoorlians, making imposing gestures towards each other before banging on the front storm shutters. That had to be scary for anyone left down below.

"Maybe we need to hide," Lion whispered.

Orchid nodded, offering, "We could go down to the shipbuilding yard, lend a hand. They may have heat-seeking scanners with them, but they have trouble with underground areas."

"Great," Tamara started issuing orders, "Alright. Everyone, hold hands. We never know when the light may go." She raised an eyebrow at Orchid, who reluctantly took her arm and started towards the stairs. It would be a long way down. Tommy reached for Lion's hand and then took Tamara's, making sure his backpack was securely strapped on.

Chapter Twenty-Nine
Fighting the Enemy

The way down was long and dark. Some of the stairwell bulbs had gone out, maybe damage, possibly because they had not been designed for such long term use. There was trash littering some of the levels, perhaps from people hiding out in here. Again Tommy wondered just how many levels of this building he never would have seen had things stuck to the usual.

Leading the way, Orchid swung onis flashlight about, and Tommy used his wrist lamps to light the back of the line-up. Their steps thudded on the concrete stairwell. Just behind him, Lion and Tamara closed the ranks.

Still, it was a treacherous walk, and there was a pause whenever they heard something. On some levels, they could hear alien sounds, speaking in their strange language, rummaging through things.

"They've gotten in," whispered Lion.

"Very likely," Tamara whispered. "The shutters were designed for storms, not security. Once you figure out how to lift them, they're literally just window dressing. If they can't hear us, we should be safe."

"Unlikely," Orchid breathed, "they won't hear us as long as we don't talk too much. They're making quite a bit of noise themselves."

"Yeah," Tommy said at a normal volume, then clasping his hand to his mouth, he whispered. "Sorry."

"Just keep moving," Orchid hissed, speeding up. There was more noise of soldiers on the third floor. As they approached the third-floor landing, the stairwell door was thrown open as a body flew, slamming into the storm shutters opposite.

A young Lhoorlian, disoriented after being thrown into the shutters, blinked at them then made a loud noise of happiness, running towards them. The sound made Tommy feel sick for a moment. That unadulterated joy at having something to kill. Orchid reacted first, grabbing both handrails propelling oniself forward with a jump, delivering a swift kick to the Lhoorlian's chest before pushing off the railing. Onis weight carrying on and landing on top of the alien. Then with a hiss, on uttered a quick sentence in the feared language. Orchid violently punching the soldier's lights out. On then stood up and made onis way back after peeking out the door to the stairwell.

Calamity at Cattori V

"His friends won't be far away," Orchid calmly said. "Let's go. They may not have heard us so-"

"Orchid Spira! Using severe violence inside the CCC is a Warning- level offence." Belinda's artificial voice boomed out, just outside the staircase. If they hadn't been heard, now they would be.

"Belinda! Silent mode!" Tamara called out. Too late, chittering laughter could be heard as another group approached the stairs. They ran fast on all fours, and Tommy spotted some shadows. Impossible to make out how many of them there were.

"Great. Thanks, Belinda," Orchid said. "I'm going to rip that thing's core out one day."

This time the AI didn't respond, at least. Sighing. Tommy activated his outfit - better to have some kind of protection than to be caught out like this. Sliding the helmet on, listening for any more movement as Orchid joined his side, standing in front of the others.

"You with me?" Tommy asked, looking over at the pink-haired one.

"I made you, and you are mine to end," Orchid replied. Tommy recoiled a bit, Orchid blinking when on noticed. "Sorry, it's an anarchist saying. I don't mean it literally." On took a deep breath, "Rest of you, keep going!"

Orchid threw onis wind up torch at Tamara.

Lion blinked, "Tommy... Those things will tear you from limb to limb."

"Maybe," he admitted, "But I can help, so I can't just run away." Seeing the aliens approaching, he barked out, "Now go so I don't have to worry about you!"

There were only two of them, though really there was no such thing as only two when it came to these beasts. Taking a deep breath and adopting a fighting stance as Orchid had taught him. His unlikely mentor giving a slight nod of approval, taking the same pose. With relief, he heard the others running away as both of them advanced through the door the alien had busted through. This floor seemed to be a service floor, with big windows but no real furniture - just a lot of older machines.

"Use the throwing knives. Even if you don't hit." Orchid instructed, and Tommy nodded. His accuracy with them wasn't great, but he was quick. Grabbing them, aiming for a moment, before tossing them with a quick flick of his wrists. One knife got a Lhoorlian right in the eye, while the other knife missed completely. Even so, if the injured Lhoorlian lagged behind, they had a better chance of taking them both out. One at a time made for much better odds. The non-injured Lhoorlian hesitated a moment but then sped up.

Orchid had once told him that Lhoorlian soldiers were taught not to fear injury, to the point where they would fight among themselves if there was nobody to fight. They had probably interrupted one such sparring match, which was frowned upon by commanders.

Likely this group had retreated to a floor with nobody else present to fight their frustrations out. But how many could be in the building in total? He had to remind himself to just worry about the two rushing towards him now. Well, one running towards him. The second would make it at some point or simply get lost entirely. He hoped for the second.

"So, what now, Orchid?"

"What, you're expecting a plan? Just take them out. Use the taser, maximum power output. These things don't go down easily, and we want to finish this fight before the other one near us wakes up."

Tommy glanced at the young one just beyond the door in the stairwell, "Gotcha." Launching a stun bolt at the alien approaching, full power as instructed. The brute staggered with the impact falling to one knee, drooling as he tried to control his body and not go down completely. Unfortunately, he found the source of his pain and grabbed the bolt, intending to pull it out. Tommy didn't hesitate and fired another one, near the neck this time. The thing tensed up as both voltage loads hit simultaneously. This time he did go down and did not look like he would get up soon.

However, the other one was finding his bearings towards the small group. He did not seem happy about his injury.

"Out of bolts!" Tommy yelled out.

"Well, don't let him find out!" sighed Orchid, seeing the alien grin as it charged towards them. This time Orchid let him come close before kicking him square in the nuts. It yelled out in Lhoorlian, and Orchid replied in kind, making the alien go wide-eyed.

Switching back to Terran, "What, think you're the only Lhoorlian bastard on this planet?"

Orchid grinned before kicking the alien in the face and retrieving the throwing dagger. Switching back to Lhoorlian and yelling something. Tommy didn't know it was possible, and maybe it was just Orchid's accent, but it sounded almost peaceful.

The alien replied bitingly, backing up submissively, but a quick glance to the side gave him away. Tommy quickly stepped in front of Orchid and hit the second alien squarely in the face, hard enough to hear his nose crack.

"Ugh." He looked over and pushed the alien away just as the retreating one jumped on his back. The alien tried to bite him, and something warm drizzled over his neck and back.

It bit me—my jugular. I'm bleeding out, panic tightening his chest, I'm going to die. But he didn't feel himself grow weaker. If anything, the alien on his back was sliding off. He turned around to see Orchid holding the throwing knife covered in blood. The blood had come from the alien's sliced throat, not his.

Calamity at Cattori V

"Remind me not to piss you off. Again." Tommy gasped as he reeled.

"Don't worry. You won't piss me off too much. Get the stun bolts out of that one. We may need them later."

Tommy sighed but pulled the bolts out anyway, wiping them on the out cold alien's shirt, which made Orchid snort. Probably because he was covered in blood.

"Blood will make the stun gun block up," Tommy huffed and reloaded the bolts. "Jeeze. Let's get down to the others before something else happens." He closed and locked the door behind them before running down the stairs.

Orchid shrugged but followed.

Lion looked up when they entered and sighed. "Fuck. You're here!" He paused nervously, looking behind them. "Are they...?"

"Nope," Tommy offered, "Well, one might be dead. The other two were locked out and aren't coming after us if they know what's good for them."

Orchid nodded in agreement before explaining somberly, "If we're lucky, they won't look for backup on the way down."

"Ray of sunshine, you are," Violet said, walking over rubbing her hands clean with a rag. "We've not had any trouble down here yet. The turrets are doing the job just fine for any that haven't found a way in or were missed during the day. I also, um, have a bit of an idea." Violet looked around, especially at Tamara.

"I'll take it. What is it?" Sighed Tamara.

"In the morning, we will hopefully have a few dead Lhoorlians. If the ones who survive leave, there will be some of their ships left down here."

Orchid nodded along, "They won't retrieve them if they think the planet will be theirs in a matter of hours."

"Then we can just grab them and run," agreed Tamara. "Scout them first, but if they come out clean, get some people on them. We've got people split up in groups with a pilot each."

"How different are Lhoorlian ships?" Asked Violet.

Orchid thought for a moment, "Our ships are capable of speed of light travel. If you navigate them below that speed, you should be fine as is. The faster than light travel requires a lot of complex calculations."

"I'd try it," Violet shrugged.

"And stop saying ours," Lion glared over at Orchid, "Whose side are you on?"

Tommy was sick of this and dryly added, "You could ask the Lhoorlian whose blood I'm wearing. I need to go wash this off somehow."

"What he said," Orchid smirked a little. "I'm with him until he's off the planet. If I'm here and you're gone, I'm joining the Lhoorlians."

"At least you're honest," said Lion in resigned tones.

"I'm not dying as a human loving idiot," Orchid said. "And dying in battle is much better than any Earth prison."

Lion bit back, "I bet you'd rather skip out on all of that inconvenience?"

"You can stop squabbling," sighed Tommy. "Is there any water down here?" He had tried a few doors as they fought, but he felt foolish feeling around in the dark. There was scant light, some from outside and the dim emergency lighting.

"We have a shower right down there," answered Violet gesturing down the corridor before pulling her eyes off Lion and Tommy. She glanced back as if she felt weird not defending Lion in this fight, turning to show Tommy the way.

"Thanks," said Tommy following her as she walked him to a large walk-in shower.

Violet pointed at a door, "The uh, employee change room also has a washer and dryer. It's right through there. Not exactly the executive washroom, but...." She shrugged.

The damp room was eerily lit by a few led strips, with a row of showers without cubicles. The tiling was a white and green checkerboard pattern which irked him for some reason.

He started by taking the armoured bits off and rinsing them off under the water before putting them aside carefully, then stepped into the water to rinse all blood off the fabric parts.

"So... This is your full get up?" She licked her lips.

"Yeah, Orchid designed it. No clue how on managed to make it." Standing under the shower, he could see the water running somewhat clear. Peeling off the tight body fabric and washing the blood and grime off before walking out the shower to toss the clothes into the washer.

Violet looked on, "Seems comfortable."

Realising then, he should probably mind that he was being watched, walking around naked. But it didn't really seem to matter right now. Wrapping a towel around himself and walking to the employee change room, stuffing everything into the washer and turning it on. At least he wouldn't smell like dried blood. Orchid had told him once Lhoorlians navigate blood like sharks and come for any target they think is injured. The last thing he wanted was to be sniffed out by a Lhoorlian while they were hiding.

The washing machine thunked into action and started a sonic clean cycle. Tommy watched it for a while then turned to head out, but Violet had already left. Perhaps for the better. He raided some shampoo and body wash from the lockers and headed back to repeat his shower. Somehow, he still felt like he smelled of blood.

Chapter Thirty

Some Rest at Last

The mood was still grim as he came back to the group. Violet had left him some clean clothes – a simple pair of jogging pants and a sweater. Orchid seemed to have taken the time to clean up as well – on wore a similar outfit and seemed none too pleased about it. On had lived the life of a rich person here. Perhaps that was why on didn't want to return? No. It didn't fit. He'd never seen on happier than when on was ripping someone apart. On wanted to fight.

Much like a Lhoorlian, on would highly likely turn against his own side when there was nobody left to fight, which made on supremely dangerous. The pink-haired fighter was very skilled in what on did. The lavish lifestyle had perhaps been more of a distraction.

Cerebellum was rumoured to have designed a life for everyone who arrived, based on what they needed to remain motivated and willing to play a part in their new society. Perhaps the AI had considered the lavish lifestyle for Orchid. Keeping on occupied with things like a large garden and pods.

Calamity at Cattori V

Maybe.

Shaking the thought out of his head. None of it mattered now. Orchid had already told him on would be on their side until he was off the planet, and he planned on being one of the last.

"Anything new?" Tommy asked to break the silence.

"No," Tamara sighed, rubbing the sides of her head. "Five of our ships have taken off without incident. Most of the non-essential personnel has been evacuated from the building, and I can't wait to take off either."

He merely nodded, surprised she was still here. Perhaps a misguided sense of loyalty that she should go down with the ship.

Lion asked, "Any way we can see if there are any other Lhoorlians in the building?"

"No. Without enough light, the cameras are useless," Violet said, looking up from a screen. "Belinda is focussed on this area alone now, which frees enough resources. We may be able to scan for heat signatures, but only the ground floor has those scanners. So at least we'll be able to scan once in a while to see if any are coming down."

Lion sighed. "Better than nothing."

"Sun is setting," Orchid said. "They'll be coming now."

"Just what we need," Tamara said. "Well. It can't be helped. Orchid and Tommy. Take turns guarding that door. Violet, keep doing whatever you're doing. You're doing it brilliantly. Lion, work out with Belinda how many people are left and how many ships we'll need. Not counting on the Lhoorlian ships just in case."

Lion nodded, "Gotcha."

Violet winked suggestively, "Always nice to be appreciated."

Tommy couldn't help but feel like her flirting hid some major fear. Selfishly, he was glad for that. It was easier to keep it together when everyone else was doing so. Tamara distributed some rations which they all tore into. Adrenaline had kept hunger pangs at bay so far.

He looked over to the others. Tamara was almost thriving under this pressure, although the cracks were starting to show. She was tired, and errors would happen if this stress continued for much longer. He did a mental inventory on himself and found himself pretty much exhausted.

"I need to sleep." It came out hoarsely out of his throat. "I'll just be in a corner. Wake me up in a few." He crumpled the packaging and threw it in something that at least resembled a bin.

Orchid nodded. "I can take first guard. I'll wake you up in three hours."

Right now, three hours sounded like paradise to the tired man.

Chapter Thirty-One
Defending a Position

Sleep came at once for Tommy, but it was a restless sleep. At least it would be over soon, and if he made it to a ship, he would be able to sleep there, safe in the knowledge there weren't any aliens to attack them. Orchid poked him, he woke up.

"My turn?" Tommy groaned. Someone had left a blanket over him, and his arm was numb from sleeping on it.

Orchid dropped the combat outfit on him as on growled, "No. You slept for two hours and a bit. There's a group of them approaching, and I'll need your help." Curt and to the point.

Slipping on the outfit, still smelling of the dryer - a strangely comforting smell in all of this. Still groggy from the sleep, but it had been better than nothing, at least.

Rubbing his face warm, Tommy felt his brain starting up. He asked, "How many?"

"Six," Orchid reported. "I could have taken them out on my own, but I wanted to be safe."

Tommy was well aware Orchid could have handled the intruders, but if on went down fighting, there would be nobody to warn them if on was overwhelmed. Yup, Orchid was nothing if not an intelligent fighter.

Nodding and finishing up with the helmet, strapping it on carefully before getting up.

Tommy asked, "Where are they?"

"They got into the lobby," Orchid sighed and looked over. "They must have evaded the AI. Anyway, the best way would be to wait until we barely hear them, when they are on the other side of the building, sneak out and attack. At the very least, we'll keep them away from the basement."

Even as people slept in shifts, the machines nearby were pumping out ships as fast they could. Each spaceship took several hours to assemble, but how many they would finish wasn't exact due to material loss. At least Tamara and Lion hadn't been able to tell how many they would be able to finish. If the power went down again, that could be the end.

No pressure, none at all. Merely nodding at that and walking after Orchid as on snuck out through the door and closed it silently behind them. Walking the empty floor staring into the dark, hoping his stun gun still had enough charge, slowly getting their eyes used to the darker area. Orchid grabbed a broom and nodded at the reception desk.

Calamity at Cattori V

Nodding in understanding. On wanted to detour that way to check on the receptionist. At the very least, he might have information on the current situation.

Moving through the building, strange sounds seemed to come from all over. He hoped there weren't more unknown groups, and it just meant the intruders had split up to cover more ground. Pausing, he heard a scuffle and the sound of something hitting the ground. It seemed like they weren't the only ones covertly moving around in the dark. Waiting until it was silent, watching the reception desk, he then ran for it, feeling something fly past him. A net? They had set a trap! They knew there was someone behind the reception desk and knew that they would come to the rescue.

One deep breath. It had missed, probably because of the dark. Circling the desk and glancing around the back of it. Luckily, the desk had one enclosed side and the wall. Easy to defend. The counter was tall, with easily enough room to hide under.

"Pst! Here!" A man's voice beckoning him closer.

"Shht!" Tommy hissed, sliding behind the desk, introducing himself softly, "I'm Tommy. Orchid's here as well."

"I know who you are. I'm Darrack," he answered, closing his eyes briefly before continuing, "They've been here for almost fifteen minutes. Why aren't they coming out?"

"Sorry to say, Darrack. You're bait. They tried to nail me as I came over." Peeking out to see if he could signal Orchid, but his backup had already vanished out of sight. He wasn't going to pop his head over the counter to get a better view. On could take care of oniself.

"Shit," Darrack swore before asking with a chuckle, "So what's their plan? Wait and see who comes out for me because it'll only be you?"

"It's a sport. They're probably bored with whatever they're doing here," Tommy explained softly, taking in a deep breath and checking the power levels on his stun gun. Half charge, would that be enough?

"Darrack, does the desk still have power?"

"Yes," nodded Darrack. "It uh, it's a small self-contained hub with a large battery that powers the doors and our computers here, mostly for security. Why?"

"Even vigilantes need a charge once in a while." Smirking and pulling out a cable to plug in his central battery to charge. The more charge, the better the range on his stun gun and the brighter his flashlights. Sighing as the little indicator light blinked briefly acknowledging the connection, then went dim. Stealth mode. Venturing a few careful peeks over the desk before dropping down again. It was quiet.

"Where's your friend?" asked Darrack, glancing around nervously.

Calamity at Cattori V

"Don't worry. On knows what on's doing." Suddenly, the sound of glass crashing, a cry, and a stomping sound. Orchid cursed loudly in Lhoorlian, before the fighting noises started up again. Darrack and Tommy tensed up, looking at one another, then it went quiet.

As soon as the quiet lasted long enough, they both peeked over the desk together. Orchid had stacked two of the Lhoorlians and was snarling at something – hopefully the third.

"Yup. Orchid is doing juuust fine," checking the suit charge. Still not very good but better than before. Pulling the cable out of the port and jumping the counter. A Lhoorlian rushed him. Quickly flashing torchlight into its eyes, making it falter and stumble. Kicking it right in the stomach, pushing it towards Orchid, who looked ready to add this one to the pile as well.

Orchid snarled into the alien's face, something that would have made Tommy crap his pants if it had been aimed at him. Watching as Orchid brutally cracked the alien's spine before throwing him on the pile, he felt a brief sense of unease. Although he was glad to have this heap of anger on his side, none of this seemed to be the work of a good person. He looked away and took a deep breath.

"Three left," he said, not just to reassure himself but to clear his mind of the sound of that horrendous shrieking. Both of them were breathing heavily.

Orchid nodded, picking onis broom back up, "They may have fled." The sudden switch from snarling mass to a reasonable person was jarring. Tommy wasn't so sure. Turning on the torch, sweeping the beam across the room. Hard edged shadows cast from pillars and doorways. It would be easy to hide here, so why wouldn't they take advantage of that?

Spotting where the aliens had ripped open a storm shutter and came in. It was a small hole and would be easy enough to patch if they could get the aliens sorted out first. Closing the gap would be easy enough, but they'd have to find a way of carrying out the Lhoorlians before they could do that. It wouldn't be safe if the aliens were lying around here, healing up and readying themselves for the next attack.

"So which way-" He was asking as a Lhoorlian interrupted, dropping onto him from above. The large CCC sign hanging above which stated their goal to be kind swayed and almost yanked out the ceiling from the sudden movement of the alien jumping off it. Falling to the floor with the alien, he had to try and gain the upper hand, rolling on top and hitting the soldier in the face. Pinning the neck with his elbow, he went to strike again, hesitating, noticing this one was female. She proceeded to bite him square in the pinning arm. Hissing in pain, he hit her squarely in the face and moved off her before blasting a stun gun bolt into her thigh.

Calamity at Cattori V

"Two more!" Tommy corrected.

"Yes," Orchid said, wiping onis brow with the back of onis hand, having broken a sweat with onis fighting. "I need an outfit like yours. These damn sweatpants are not that great."

"It's what people wear to exercise." Tommy shrugged and glanced over. "They don't look terrible on you if that's what you're worried about."

"Yes, Tommy. I'm very worried about how my butt looks in these pants as I'm roundhouse kicking the race of people I used to fight a war against." Orchid sighed, looking around, "Keep scanning the area. Is the man okay?"

"Yeah. Darrack's fine and hiding," He nonchalantly added, glancing around as he moved the beam across. "What if the two others fled?"

"Stop being so optimistic," bit back Orchid, pushing onis back against Tommy's in an attempt to cover them both.

"Just saying. We're kicking ass here." Finishing his 360-degree check of the room, "Nothing."

"Right." Orchid's shoulders relaxing a little, but only a little. Onis back was still firmly pressed against him, and they kept turning slowly, torchlight dancing across the room's walls. Staying silent, ears and eyes open for any movement. So far, there was none.

This continued for another minute before Tommy relaxed and turned the suit lights to a lower setting, eager to conserve battery.

"Right," Orchid said, finally breaking the silence, "They probably fled or are hiding. Either way. I wouldn't go back down just yet."

"You just told them where we are!" Tommy hissed.

"They don't speak Terran! Jeeze," Orchid sighed, "You humans think everyone speaks Terran."

"Last I checked, you were human as well."

"You know what I mean!" Orchid exasperated, looking around. "Plus, there's probably some Lhoorlian in my DNA after all those generations," on let out a deep sigh, "They might be gone." Lowering the broom, on was holding when there was another scuffling sound, this time towards the desk.

"There!" Tommy shouted.

A dark shape was running from the wall towards the desk, which stood between them. Tommy dashed towards it, rushing over to the desk. Darrack was still there. Hopefully, he could reach Darrack before the alien. There was a good twenty meters between them, and even in the dark, their trajectories were quite clear. They weren't directly opposite. Making a snap judgement, he started running straight at the alien, trying to cut it off.

Orchid sprinted past, swinging the broom from on high onto the alien's head. The Lhoorlian cried out and turned towards them, trying to grab the broom. This one was taller than the other ones, with longer claws and a pair of goggles on its face, nightvision? Tommy immediately flashed his torch into the alien's face as he saw that, happy to use that to his advantage.

The Lhoorlian screeched and hurled off the night vision goggles, blinking to get his vision back. Orchid didn't wait, smacking him directly in the face with the broom. The sound of a bone breaking made Tommy wince. He would never have used that much force, but this was not a game. These aliens would kill them if given half a chance.

A noise behind him, he called out, "I hear the other one!"

"Don't go too far!" Orchid ordered.

But it was too late. From the balconies above, another two aliens dropped in the space between them. One was shorter, male, blood matting in his hair and a wild look in his eyes. He couldn't see the tall one behind the wild one very well, but it appeared equally angry about the current state of affairs. These three had apparently worked out this tactic to split them up, and they were putting it into motion.

Licking his lips and backing up, hoping to separate them a bit. The two of them working together would be tough to beat. Hearing the thwack of the broom handle as Orchid fought, feeling he should follow Orchid's lead and not give the aliens too much thinking time. Lashing out, jabbing the short wild one in the jaw with his left fist, unbalancing him before following it up with an uppercut. Unbalanced, the alien still managed to dodge the second blow, bounding into his partner behind him.

"Hah!" He grinned, glad he had some distance, his best weapon was the stun gun, and with the knowledge of the last encounter, he quickly fired two bolts. The bolts landed. The short wild alien snarled before being shocked into unconsciousness. Little red battery shape blinked in his helmet display, end of the line for his battery.

Orchid let out a gasp as the other alien grabbed on by the hair, forcing on into a chokehold. The tall alien barked something.

Orchid gasped, "He's saying to take him to our leader."

"What's "fat chance" in Lhoorlian?" Tommy replied immediately. He would rather not lose Orchid, but if that was the only option to keep the others safe, that would be worth it.

"I don't think we have anything like that."

"Great, translation issues on top of this!" Rolling his eyes and sighing. How would he take out this alien, without a stun gun, without power, and other unconscious aliens who could recover in minutes?

Suddenly, a shot rang out. And then a second as the first seemed to have missed.

Calamity at Cattori V

Orchid kicked the alien's shin and pulled loose as on fell to the floor. Turning, he saw Darrack behind him holding a gun, shakily. Darrack was wearing the night vision goggles the alien had discarded earlier, giving him a better idea of where to shoot, at least.

"I had no idea this worked," stammering Darrack explained, "Tamara left me with this one. I thought it was against looters." Dropping it with a soft cry. Tommy walked over.

"You did good," reassuring the receptionist, who seemed in shock. The first shot seemed to have grazed Orchid, but the second had gone through the alien's thigh. He was down and out for the count and perhaps even bleeding to death.

"Let's go downstairs," Orchid said through gritted teeth, clutching onis arm and spitting at the Lhoorlians, yelling something in their language.

"What was that?" asked Tommy. Prodding the stunned receptionist forward, he took Darrack's handgun.

"Peace or annihilation," Orchid said after a moment's thought. "It's the imperialist slogan."

"I thought you were not an imperialist?"

"No, but we want any Lhoorlian coming after us to believe that, so when the imperialists leave their ships, they leave us alone. Or leave me alone. I don't know what they'll do to you."

"Such a way with people you have," Tommy remarked in disbelief, rushing towards the door to the basement. Without their torches, they were at a disadvantage, especially with Darrack. The light from Orchid's torch was dimming, probably the battery running low. Dimming his own torch and just checking once in a while to make sure they were still on track. Putting distance between themselves and the aliens.

Finally, they made it, Tommy banging on the door until Violet opened it, covering them with a shotgun. Good choice of weapon, Tommy thought. It could do some real damage up close. He shoved Darrack in first and then let Orchid in before closing the door behind them.

The factory floor was warm and well lit, and Violet and two workers were guarding the door. Violet handed the shotgun to one of them, then notepad and remotes in her arms rushed over.

"Are you alright?" Violet glancing over their injuries.

"No!" Orchid declared, "Little dick over there shot me."

"It grazed," Tommy said, frustrated and crouching down, warming his hands before putting them on the bullet wound. This time, however, the familiar tingle didn't happen. Fuck.

Orchid looked at him for a moment before pulling onis arm away, "I think it's not only your suit batteries which are empty. Go back to sleep."

"Yeah, right." Resigned and tired, sleep would come fast enough. While some adrenalin still pumped from the run, keeping him moving, he started dealing with the small stuff. Popping the battery out of the suit, he plugged it into a wall socket to charge. Taking inventory, it seemed like he would be awake forever, his heart rate still up. The short nap earlier had already been forgotten. Then when he did finally put his head down, it didn't take very long before he drifted away.

Chapter Thirty-Two
The Wrong Choice

Waking up as the sun rose, and for a moment, the world seemed okay. There was a smell of food, people chatted, and even Orchid seemed pleasant, snoring nearby. Drooling on a mat a metre or so away, on had onis top off, revealing a chest full of scars he had seen so many times before while training. A quick bandage had been strapped around onis arm. Violet sat nearby on a supply crate working.

"Morning..." he said, blinking away the sleep. "They left us alone?"

Violet smiled brightly, "Lion and I went out with Orchid to repair the hole in the shutters. We hooked them up to a car battery, so they were electrified. Seemed to help even if the voltage is just very low."

"I guess they're not used to our kind of electricity," snickered Tommy looking around the room for the source of the food smell. "What's cooking?"

Calamity at Cattori V

"Just rations," Lion said. "We're frying some spam, so it at least has some taste."

He hated spam, but now it actually seemed worthy of breakfast. There appeared to be a certain excitement in the air. Perhaps because no matter what, it would soon be over, and it would be unlikely there would be another night like this. They would either be on a ship off of this planet, or they would be dead. Either would be preferable to cowering in the dark, trying to operate on little sleep.

"Are you still going with the captured ship plan?" Tommy asked, feeling a little bit guilty he had slept in this long and determined to get up to speed as fast as possible again.

"Yep!" Violet grinned and looked over, "You can come if you want. Someone to watch our backs is always handy. But... We can go on our own."

Looking from Violet to Lion, who was standing at the stove. Lion and his sister seemed to have such a good, simple bond, understanding each other quickly.

He nodded. "Yeah, I'll come after breakfast." He checked his suit battery status, pretty sure he wouldn't be changing out of the outfit until they were off the planet. It was coming along nicely, but it wouldn't be fully charged for another hour or so.

The sunlight coming in through the vents was wonderful, warming the basement up as they worked. Tamara and Darrack were speaking in hushed tones by a pile of paperwork. Tommy wandered over to them, feeling he would not be as helpful at the cooking station, "Morning."

"Hey," Tamara sounded grim. "We got the footage from outside. They bombed some of the larger buildings during the night. One bomb hit a ship."

Tommy felt his stomach dropping. He tried asking if anyone was hurt, but the first syllable stuck in his throat.

"Yeah," Darrack nodded, answering the unasked question. "It was one of ours. Full of people. No survivors that we can tell."

Tommy should have known something like this would happen, but it still shocked him through to his core. Even after all the fighting, this seemed to make it more real. More tangible. And he was madder than ever. His fists clenched by his sides as he looked away, asking, "So. What do we do now?"

"We stick to the plan," Tamara frowned. "The plan is our best shot of getting as many people as possible off the planet. It didn't look like they were bombing ships intentionally, so we can only assume it was hit by accident. Perhaps this tragedy can deliver us with a cease-fire for a few hours."

"They are not really attacking during the day, so it's just a few hours to midnight we need to clear." Tommy nodded, trying to keep his mind clear. Emotions would cloud it. His training had taught him that much. If he went numb and lost hope now, it would be the worst possible outcome for everyone.

As small a part as he played, they needed him. They needed Tamara, they needed Lion, they needed Violet, they needed Darrack, and they definitely needed Orchid.

He nodded, "It's worth a shot once Orchid is up. On is the one who can talk to them."

Violet glanced over to the snoring man, "Can we trust on?"

Tommy sighed. "We can as far as onis life depends on it," he looked over at the sleeping warrior. "Peace or annihilation. He said that was one of their slogans, the imperialists." He didn't know if that tidbit of information would help, but maybe, just maybe, it would.

"I've heard that before," Tamara confirmed. "They ended their message with that when they offered us the ships."

"Good sign, then?" Perhaps too early to get optimistic, but it was better than nothing. Glancing around, he saw Orchid slowly waking up.

Tommy walked up to the rigged up cooker and smiled, "Spam never smelled this good."

"Yup," Lion said proudly as he stirred in some sauce, "Found some garlic powder and cans of tomato in one of the supply cabinets. Should be okay on a bit of the wonderbread we pilfered. Thank goodness some of our coworkers kept their lunches in their lockers."

Tommy laughed, "You stole it? Wow."

"Anyone who keeps garlic powder and canned tomato in their locker deserves to have their lockers robbed, Tommy." Lion flipped the spam, pouring more tomato on top. The smells didn't lie. It might actually taste okay.

Tommy chuckled at the casual office joke, "To be fair, the tomatoes were probably from my groceries." It had been a whirlwind since the incident with the pickup. It was hard to believe it had been less than a month since all that had happened. Life had gone off the rails, but not just for him. An entire planet had their lives turned upside down. Somewhere, that had to take a toll on everyone. He took a deep breath as Lion worked the sauce into the dish.

"Get the bread, will you?" Lion asked, nodding at the plastic bag of bread they had found. It would be little food for all six of them but better than nothing. He plated the slices, ready to receive the saucy load and nodded to Lion.

"Thanks for this. It's... Wonderful to have some food."

"Yeah," Lion agreed while scooping warm sauce and spam mixture up on some of the bread. "Try some. It might be horrid."

"I'm sure we won't keel over," taking a careful bite of the saucy bread and meat mix, "Not bad." Within moments, he had finished the sandwich. The tangy warmth was doing him a load of good.

"Good," said Lion, glancing over. It was then he remembered they hadn't really been alone in a while, and he wasn't sure if he wanted to be. Violet was not too far away, grabbing whatever she could to arm herself on her upcoming trip out to the abandoned ships. He quickly shouted over to her, "Violet, when do we leave?"

Violet looked up, "An hour max. We've got eyes outside trying to find ships, so we know where we're going, but if we can't find anything that way, it'll be up to us. If you see anything useful like alien or local electronics, grab them, but don't weigh yourself down. We may have to make a run for it."

"How will we get any ships here?" He wondered.

"The pods. They have trailer beds, but they're in the car yard. We'll need to attach them, and then we'll head out. I'm just hoping they'll have enough power to drag the ships to our side of the yard."

"Those things run for very long distances with a full charge," agreed Tommy.

"Far, yes, but the towing power? I'm sure it does great with two people, but what about four? What about when it's hooked up to a spaceship five times its size?" She shook her head. "This whole plan could easily be a failure, but we have to try."

Tommy nodded along to her words. She was right. Even if it did fail at worst, they had inspected some ships.

"Can I ask a favour? If we can't get the ships close, would it be possible to get people to them?" Tommy asked.

"Broadcasting their location or whatever?"

"Possibly," Violet tentatively answered, raising an eyebrow and taking a sandwich from Lion. After a bite, she clarified, "But... It could be dangerous."

"For some of these people, it might be their only chance." Tommy took stock of their group. Their little squad was in the know, but he still didn't know that much. Ships were being pumped out and prepped for launch thanks to automated mechanisms. He had no clue if they were filled to the brim or mostly empty. Not a pleasant journey to sleep in cramped barracks for a few years, but better than dying to alien soldiers on a prison planet. Violet finished devouring the sandwich while he grabbed his suit's battery, thinking through the problem.

He sighed and headed for the stairs, "I'll go check which vehicles have a charge and bring them around. Since we lost the mains, there might only be a few pods with a full charge left."

"Be careful," prompted Violet, wiping crumbs from her mouth. "Lion! Go with him, for fuck's sake." She made a face.

Lion, rolling his eyes, finished handing out the last few sandwiches. "Fine! But only to scout the vehicles. I don't do that fancy fighting stuff."

"Kicking at anything that moves is good enough," Tommy sighed, not looking forward to being alone with him again. Maybe a little. The kiss had been nice. But what could come of that right now?

He shook his head at the thought and walked out towards the yard, waiting for Lion to follow him.

"Wait up," Lion called, catching up fully. The shutters' patched hole was still there. The car battery hooked to the jagged edge of the metal by crocodile clips. Sunlight came through, lighting calm dust motes in the air with warm beams. In a kind of the-world-is-still-there way, though that was perhaps for not much longer.

Disconnecting the battery, then lifting the shutters, it only rolled partway before jamming. As expected. Rollers got stuck on buckled and bent metal from the damage which caused the hole. Looking through the gap, he made sure the area outside was secure, then nodded for Lion to go through first. Lion climbed through and then waited for him.

Outside, it was a hot day. Dry. Sunny. It would have been beautiful if not for the bodies of both humans and Lhoorlians lying around.

Lion gagged and needed a moment to steady himself. "Fuck. People went out and tried to fight those things?"

Some were indeed holding makeshift weapons. Kitchen knives, mostly, a few guns perhaps raided from guards. One was holding a bat made out of a piece of plywood.

"When people are cornered..." Tommy shook his head. "They fight back. They probably thought that was the best course of action. We know a lot more about them than others. Don't forget we didn't know it was an invasion for the longest time."

Lion sighed, "This way." He turned to head for the yard, where the pods stood untouched, mostly. Dusty from the explosions and destruction, but virtually unchanged otherwise. Tommy cleaned the dust off the windshield of the first one then got in to check the charge. While doing his check, he told Lion, "Check the charge, turn off right away. If they're not fully charged, we take the battery with us." Pulling out a marker and drawing a tick, he took out a second one and gave it to Lion. "Mark any pod with over 90% charge with a tick mark and a circle if you take the battery out."

At the very least, Violet would be able to do something creative with them even if they didn't make it work for a pod. Power was still power. Electricity would work for whatever it was they needed it for.

Nodding Lion took the pen and looked at the yard. Lion then pointed at the pods on the right-hand side and starting to walk off. Tommy groaned, giving a thumbs up, reluctantly agreeing to do all the pods on the yard's left side. They would need to split up to make sure that they covered everything as fast as possible. Time was of the essence. Still, the thought of Lion crossing a Lhoorlian soldier without him within striking range was rather... problematic.

Sighing but walking to his side, he looked around. A thick bush line, well maintained, fenced off the yard from the

Calamity at Cattori V

outside, protecting from intruders. The sound in the yard was deadened, but there didn't seem to be anyone there. If the pods weren't seen, it was easier to keep them safe, he guessed. He walked to the second pod on the left, opened it and slid inside.

No luck. It was completely dead. Getting out, drawing a circle on the glass, seeing it had been connected to charge. Probably been plugged in just moments before the power went down. How bad was the power outage? Was it just here, he wondered, or was it the entire planet? The whole world trying to run on generators. Not a great thought.

He glanced up at the sky as another spaceship streaked the clear blue dome and then turned back to what he was doing. People were still getting out but no time to waste. Shifting from pod to pod, he would climb in on one side, do his checks, then exit on the other side, all to minimise walking. Seventy percent. He got out, marked a circle, and popped the hood, disconnecting the battery quickly. They had been designed to last and be easy to service, so it was just a matter of popping the leads off the battery and lifting it out quickly. Placing the battery down in front of the pod, he would pick it up on the way back. These things were heavy, and transporting them down the stairs would not be easy.

He took a deep breath and rushed over to the third pod. This time he was lucky. The engine started with a roar and displayed a 98 percent charge. Beautiful! He clapped his hands and marked the car with a large tick mark before listening for Lion. There was still a sound of pod doors being opened and closed. Climbing on top of the pod, he could see Lion going through the cars faster than he was. No time to waste then.

Hopping from the roof of the pod, he had just finished checking to the next one and slid down the smooth exterior, taking a deep breath. How many pods would be okay for their endeavour, he wondered. It was not like this would be an easy job either way. Checking the battery with a sigh and shaking his head. Twenty percent, was it worth grabbing the battery? He scribbled a circle onto the front and then took out the battery and carried it to the first battery. This time, Lion met him during the battery-run.

"Six more to go," the taller man grinned and glanced over. "You got any luck?"

"Some," Tommy shrugged, "That one vehicle has a near full charge. Should do us most the way at least."

"If you're okay being on your own for a bit, I am going to take a battery down. See if Violet can't find a way to charge it. Hand cranking, wind, whatever. She's smart."

Tommy glanced around, evaluating. They were okay for the time being. The terrain was pretty empty of Lhoorlians, and the aliens inside the building were either dead or long gone. It was very likely that the Lhoorlians had just picked up all their survivors and were just waiting until they could unleash everything they had on the planet.

"Yeah. Go on. But come find me before you do anything else, okay?" Their time would run out if they weren't careful. As he saw the other running off, he sat down on the hood of a pod for a second. Right now he didn't want to take his eyes off of the other.

He didn't relax until he saw Lion walking back. A rustle, but it was off to the side. Cause for concern? Maybe. His eyes wandered to his peripheral vision. Someone was running around the yard and he could not tell if it was a Lhoorlian or just a human. But right now, they were moving like a threat. Decision time. No, he didn't have all the information. But if it was a Lhoorlian...

His hand moving to pull out the stun gun, drawing down and aiming. Watching through the nib sight, the figure coming into focus. Squeezing the trigger, dart flying but narrowly missing. A cry as he ducked into cover.

"Lion! Hurry!" Tommy cried out. Lion looked around, confused, but kept his head down, running. Their voices echoed through the yard. If there were other intruders, they had just given up their position.

"I missed. Someone's out there." Checking the stun gun ammo. He peeked up. The other was still moving.

"I saw." Lion's voice moving closer.

A pod powering up. He had lost track of the target. Whoever it was, they had managed to get into a pod.

A pod was bad. It meant they would be moving a lot faster. Worse. The sound of the pod was increasing in volume which meant it was coming closer. The two of them stood in the way of the intruder and the exit.

Tommy jumps up. Pods didn't have weapons. Weapons fire was less of an issue right now. He needed to know the trajectory of the pod.

As he expected it was coming straight for them. Head strafing to find Lion. Lion had not spotted it – he looked around, trying to locate where the noise was coming from. He saw it, too late. Lion tensing up, standing straight in the path of the pod.

Memories of hot asphalt, broken glass returned to Tommy. No. He would not let Lion get hurt again.

The assisted braces clicked on as he sprinted, jumped, pushing over Lion. He'd been too far away. Inches.

The metal brace on his leg was the first thing he heard snap. After that his scream drowned out most of the noise, even that of the pod. Or had it stopped? The weight on his leg was still there. The pain was starting to filter through his disjointed thoughts, biting hard. He screamed out in pain, unable to keep it in any longer.

Lion gasped. "Get that pod off of him! What are you doing?" He pounded on the pod.

"I'm sorry! He shot at me!" The girl gasped. She sounded young. Panicked. He had made a mistake. This was not a Lhoorlian scavenger. Just a survivor who had been trying

Calamity at Cattori V

to find transport. His stomach churned.

He couldn't tell much more - his face was almost pressed into the ground as his leg was pinned.

"Are you ok?" She leaned out of the pod. A young face, tear streaks causing clear streaks on her dirty face.

"Fine," Tommy said through gritted teeth. "Get out the pod. What's the charge level on it?"

"Eighty-nine. Why?" She asked, reversing off of his leg. The pain changed as blood rushed in. The pressure was no longer there, but damn. That stung.

"At least you just did something useful," Lion huffed, annoyed and angry, he looked over at her. "So, get the fuck inside. And hope we don't die considering you just took out one of our best fighters."

"What? I don't understand. I don't understand any of this!" She seemed close to tears, getting out of the pod.

Tommy tried to sit up and found it hard to sympathise with her.

"By midnight, this planet will be taken over or destroyed by a hostile alien race which is almost unkillable. If you're lucky, we can get you off the planet." He took a deep breath and closed his eyes a moment as Lion rushed up to him.

"Oh, thank god. You're still conscious." Lion looked at the injured leg with worry evident on his face. The armour had either helped or made things a lot worse. He had no idea right now. The pain was just everything.

"I'll get you inside. Orchid and Violet can help out with the checking. Can you heal yourself?"

"No," inhaling between gritted teeth. "Fuck!" He took the helmet off.

"I thought you were a soldier in that get-up!" The young woman exclaimed. "What are you even doing on private terrain?"

"Oh for fuck's..." Lion rolled his eyes. "Surviving. What about you, smart ass?" Shaking his head in disgust. "Jeeze. You really think you're the only one scared and alone? You never are even when there aren't aliens orbiting the planet."

"Well..." She looked at him. "I'm sorry, okay?"

Tommy took the top of the outfit off. "Take it." He said to Lion. "And the helmet. Or give it to Violet. Don't give it to Orchid, or on may just take on the Lhoorlians and claim the planet for oniself."

"Monarch Orchid does have a ring to it. Help me carry him. What's your name?"

"Elizabeth," she said.

"Well, I'm Lion, and that's Tommy. And that's Tommy's broken leg, say hi!"

"I said I was sorry!"

"And I'm furious and not sure what saying how you feel about this does right now!" Lion replied and shot her a glare.

The whole thing was rather amusing to Tommy. He hadn't expected the man to get so protective over him, but it felt nice. Which meant more than anything, he had to be careful now and figure his emotions out.

He cried out when they lifted him up. "Fuck!" He whispered and whimpered in his limited vocabulary. Creative swearing wasn't a study course on a prison planet where your household AI scolds you for being a potty mouth. "Fuuuuuck!" he called out. There were definitely multiple breaks there. Not good, considering their improvised ships would barely have bunks, let alone recovery rooms. The aliens hadn't left many wounded, either way. It was just stupid humans hurting each other this time.

His mind was racing, but most likely, it was just the pain that was killing him. His good leg almost dragged on the floor, and he had to remember to bend the wounded leg and then move the good one so the two others could get him inside through the small opening of the broken shutter.

"Fuck, you're heavy," sighed Elizabeth.

"Adding literal insult to injury, huh?" Tommy croaked, trying to keep his spirits up. If he let himself go now, he would only go to a dark place where all the stuff he had not touched upon in the last twenty-four hours was waiting for him, waiting to consume him and his sanity.

"FUCK!"

"Sorry," she apologised before meekly asking, "Have you guys got food?"

Violet rushed over to them, "Jeeze! What happened up there?"

Tamara rolled up her sleeves, "I've got some triage and nurse experience. Put him down. It's a miracle none of us got hurt."

Orchid cried over, "Hey, I'm hurt."

"Barely. Isn't that stubbing your toe to a Lhoorlian?" She glanced over, and on shrugged meekly. It seemed to have hindered Orchid less than anything, to the point Tommy hadn't even thought about healing on even when he had just woken up.

"So... It looks bad." Tamara stated, raising an eyebrow, carefully untying the shoe and pulling the laces out to open it as wide as possible. "You're going to want something to bite down on."

Tommy groaned, "Suppose you don't have any cookies?"

"Not today. They haven't come out of the oven yet," she smiled and glanced over. That must have been her nurse face, as it looked very different from her face when she was in command. Much more pleasant, but much more forced as well.

Calamity at Cattori V

Lion passed something over his head—a leather belt.

"Oh, we're going for kinky now?" Tommy tried to joke.

"Open wide," Tamara put the folded belt between his teeth then removed the shoe as swiftly as she could.

He cried out and bit down on the leather, feeling like he would bite through it. The sock was less painful, rolling it off slowly, probably hadn't been holding the bones together as much. But after days of running around, it was less pleasant for other reasons.

Violet made a face as the sock was swiftly discarded. After that, it was pretty smooth sailing - with a hand from Lion, Tamara cut the leg of the pants off and peeled it off, barely touching the leg underneath. She had practice with this, he could tell. He wondered where she had accumulated it.

"Leg seems like a simple fracture. That I can set. The foot is going to need some more specialised care." She pushed her hair behind her ears and started looking around. "I need some planks or something and fabric ribbons. We have to stabilise this mess as much as possible."

Tommy spat out the belt and made a face, "That's my leg you're talking about."

"Shush. Who said you could remove that? I'm not done."

Violet walked over, handing him some pills. "I found some painkillers. This should at least help some." They were packaged in a neat pink package with a smiling woman plucking flowers. But even if they were designed to alleviate period cramps, it was better than nothing. He thrust his hand out for whatever dose she deemed correct. Tamara grabbed the box and pushed out two after reading the instructions.

"That's the max dose for six hours. You don't want constipation along with this mess."

He swallowed them dry and laid back again. Fuck. He would be out for the rest of this thing, and it hurt. He had hoped to be more useful than this! Stuck on a makeshift bed with his leg and foot broken because he hadn't been careful enough. What a disaster. All he could do now was trust the rest of them, as they had trusted him.

He winced as Tamara shoved some wood around the foot and then the leg and then carefully bandaged it all together.

"You're going to need to rest for a few months. If we could get you proper treatment, less than that. Orchid! What kind of medical facilities do Lhoorlian ships have?"

"How should I know? I've never been on one," Orchid shrugged. "I pilot trained on a simulator in the resistance, and that was only because they had captured one of those things. It wasn't the greatest."

"Blast it all," Tamara sighed. "Do you think there's any way we could steal a Lhoorlian doctor?"

He knew why she was reaching. A break in zero-g wasn't the greatest. A poorly taken care of break? The healing process depended on gravity. He'd be lucky not to have a backwards bending knee. Or similar. He had no real idea beyond the fact it was just "bad".

"Alright. Violet, Lion." Tamara ordered, "Go continue on with the pod count. I want to be able to get out of here sooner than later. Orchid. Give them back up."

Orchid shrugged and put a shirt on.

Lion put on most of the combat suit but gave the helmet to Violet.

"Gotta protect the brains." He grinned and looked over.

"Thanks." She snorted and glanced over him. "Shit! This thing is advanced!" She grinned.

Orchid sighed and walked over. "I'll give you the tutorial on your new toys as we go. Come on. Alien overlords ain't waiting for us."

Orchid started up the stairs and took a deep breath. Violet followed and waved, and then Lion closed the ranks, and they were out of sight.

At the very least, they didn't need to have the talk now. But there was very little to preoccupy Tommy other than the throbbing pain of his broken leg and foot.

Chapter Thirty-Three

Trust

As he looked out of the pod window, the last ship took off from the headquarters building they had left hours earlier. It was a beautiful sight to see it streak up. The small ship's rocket plumes streaked the sky, and they had launched at regular intervals – he only guessed this one was the last because it had taken longer. Perhaps they had looked for stragglers before taking off. Either way, he was happy to see it go.

Tommy had most of the back of a pod to himself, a luxury. Stretched out on the backseat with his busted leg. Lion and Violet sat upfront. The pods were in convoy, this pod was the one in the back, so it could follow the path smoothed out by the pods in the front. Between the vehicles, there was active radio communication so they could all remain in contact.

The road had been dull for the last hour or so. The initial destination was the alien ship, or rather the meeting spot where the alien ship would land in a few hours. After that, they would just go and scout for more spaceships. It would probably not make the best impression being handed a ship while salvageable ships were lying around the place. They were already doing them a favour by not killing them, to begin with.

The rolling scenery became more peaceful as they left the city. Dead bodies and broken building debris made space for more wildlands. Slowly being tamed by some stray terraforming machines which were tilling the soil until it grew grass enough to start growing trees. Trees meant more oxygen. It meant more life.

It just turned the planet into a more habitable place at this point. The climate was already more than agreeable enough, but the similarity to earth helped on a psychological level. Having ventured out of the cities, Tommy knew what it looked like. Lion and Violet seemed glued to the machines and the almost desert-like sand. He shook his head before clearing his throat and asking, "You guys have never left the city?"

Violet shook her head, her voice quiet, "Even the caves for the resistance weren't this far out. It's beautiful, though."

The giant machines moved lazily across the plains. Wide jaws poking, chewing holes in the soil and spitting out grass seeds and chemicals, a dried mixture that had come from earth, while the back spread out a thin mist of vapour. Self-powered and sustaining, these things had no idea what was happening to the world they had helped create. Perhaps the Lhoorlians wouldn't mind them, and they would be roaming for ages to come and make the entire planet into a green pasture. And one day, when humans could return, perhaps they would find this place a beautiful oasis, and it would be for everyone, not just convicts sent to work the land.

Or maybe he was just delirious with pain. The painkillers were not that strong and mainly had just worked for the first two hours, and he wasn't sure how long they had been driving. "How far out are we?"

Violet glanced at her screen at the coordinates they'd been given. She said, "Five clicks out if this is correct." Her gaze returns to the pods before her. "We've sent the coordinates out to everyone on radio channels to come here. This will be our launching pad in only a few short hours."

"Right." They had carried him, passed out, into the pod, so now he was trying to figure out who was where. Violet was his driver, so the other five were probably in two pods together. Maximise the number of pods. Or perhaps three pods. Who knew. He tried glancing out the back, but they had taken the rear, and he could only see the one in front of them. Behind them lay nothing but dust.

"So, how do you feel?" Violet asked after a moment, glancing behind her briefly.

"Let's just say I hope the Lhoorlians have invented painkillers already."

That seemed to make her chuckle. She replied, "Orchid said they're super advanced when it comes to science, so I have no reason to suspect they haven't." She smiled. "Especially with the number of wars they fight. They probably have a bunch of healing pods on their ship. And it'll go so much faster with their faster than light technology."

"I hadn't even thought of that." Okay, that brought a smile to his face. Three years on a ship had seemed like a far-out idea, like a possibility that would never happen. Then this morning, it had been a reality. And now, well, even just shortening the trip a bit would make an enormous difference.

"Do you look forward to earth?" She asked, and this time he guessed she was trying to keep his mind off the pain in his leg.

"Yeah. I guess. I mean. Not like I can stay, so I'm... happy to go. But also it's not really a choice. It's complicated." He shifted and winced. Perhaps not the best idea.

"At the very least, you'll have friends." She nodded and turned her gaze back to the road. Smaller groups of pods were gathering around it, but the view was still stunning.

"We're here." She stopped the car behind the others. "Holy shit."

Then there was a loud explosion, and the exclamations turned a little less enthusiastic.

"We're under fire!" Violet almost u-turned the pod, trying to get away from the leading group. Tommy almost hit the roof of the vehicle, trying to hold on to anything in the fast-moving pod. "A trap!" Violet sounded panicked.

"No." Orchid sounded over the pod intercommunication system. "They're anarchists. Not the people we're meant to meet." On sounded confident.

Tamara took over, "Break formation. We're unarmed, so the best we can do is dance around them."

Around them, sand flew up like a giant explosion. One of the terraforming machines had been hit and was leaning over.

"Violet!" Tommy cried out, hoping she saw it leaning towards them as well.

"I see it!" The pod lurched again, away from the machine but almost hitting the pod in front of them. Then it started to rain debris. Violet braked violently then turned the wheel, sending them into another direction. He was stunned by her calm and precise driving, dodging debris and pulling them clear of the area. As he watched the expert level driving, he was reminded of a lifetime ago, Lion talking about his sister, the getaway driver.

A large shadow covered the sun for a second. This was too big to dodge. This couldn't be how it ended.

The large ship above them slowly came down to land.

Chapter Thirty-Four
Happy Ending

Perhaps they wouldn't need the smaller ships all that much. The alien ship had already landed, and it looked to be about a kilometre wide and twenty or so meters high.

It was beautiful in a bizarre way. The outside looked to have triangular portholes, with the other triangles filled with art pieces reminiscent of battle scenes. It would make sense for the race to decorate their ships with the tableaus of war. The top seemed to be made of a glowing ring of light slowly moving around it, hovering just a few inches above the canopy. The ramp had been extended, but it looked to be just part of the ship. A ring around the starship with a sloping upwards incline leading into the ship's interior. Three Lhoorlians sitting on it. They didn't look like soldiers as they were wearing long robes and had long hair.

Tommy waited impatiently for Violet to help him out of the back seat. He leaned on her as they limped towards the ship.

"Wow... It's huge." His neck ached as he tried taking it all in.

Orchid shot past them and started talking to the aliens, probably for the best, as none of them would have a clue how to properly greet the emissaries.

Lion joined Violet to help hold Tommy. Lion added, "Look at that. I think we can get everyone on this."

"Yeah. Can you imagine?" Tommy said.

"Easily." Tamara's voice came from behind, "Darrack's keeping an eye on the numbers. Fifty left. We'll need a few hours to round everyone up, and if anyone's hiding, perhaps we can get them on. This complicates things, but..." She held her hands to her mouth. "We might be able to save everyone who's left."

Stepping past them, Tommy saw her biting her lip, tears streaking her face, and he was surprised to see the stoic woman shed tears of happiness. But after all of this, it had to come as a surprise. One of their first real turns to good luck.

Orchid turned to them. "These are high ranking officials for the imperialist government. They sent their biggest ship, but they ask that we put a good word in for them in return. Well, that's an understatement but a close translation."

"I can do that." Nodded Tamara, rubbing her cheeks.

"You would be taking sides in a giant conflict that has been raging for years," warned Orchid.

"And I'd be able to save many, many lives which have been entrusted to me. I can't care about the implications of those politics right now." She nipped back, and to Tommy's ears, it sounded almost Lhoorlian.

"Ask about a sickbay," Tommy chimed from his perch.

Orchid snorted and looked to the officials, exchanging a few short words.

"Yes, yes, they do." On said and looked back. "It is rudimentary, but it should heal broken bones fairly well."

The Lhoorlians stepped aside and bowed a little as a smaller space ship descended. The aliens spoke to Orchid in a slow, deliberate way as if they weren't sure on could understand. If the fighter took offence, on didn't show it. They motioned for some of the arrivals to enter up the ramp. Tamara took a step onto the ramp and looked around, uncertain, but the aliens only seemed to encourage her to step on.

"It's time for them to ...make room. There isn't much time left, but they will help us defend the ship until the ultimatum runs out," Orchid interpreted. "And... they would like for us to teach them Terran, so one of them will travel with us to learn the language. We are to treat him like one of our own, obviously. I don't think I need to expand on what would happen to us if we hurt a hair on his head."

"What's his name?" Tamara asked from the edge of the ramp.

"Ysti." The Lhoorlian smiled a little. He was the one with the longest hair in the group.

Orchid blinked and barked something back, but the man just repeated the almost upbeat, innocent little word. Ysti.

"What does that mean?" Tommy asked.

"It's a title." Orchid turned to them. "It means Emperor."

Other Works

Vade Mecum Series

Magic recently returned to the modern world. For now only few people have an inkling of how it works. One of them is the world's leading magical researcher Atze Furcifer, but he'd prefer you leave him a voicemail so he can continue ignoring you...

Join the grumpy mage on his quest to get a hot cup of tea and avoid another nasty adventure.

Game Dev | Null

Collections of slice of life doodles documenting and proving the old saying, "Truth is Stranger than Fiction". Removing the names to protect the innocent, guilty and outright bizarre. We hope these let you glimpse into fresh perspectives.

Flammable Penguins

Flammable Penguins is a small press publishing company run out of London by Claire Blackshaw and Daphné D'Haenens. With the cuddles and lack of assistance from their two cats.

https://FlammablePenguins.com/

Thank you for supporting our little dream 🖤